WOLF BLOOD

MAY 16 2012

WOLF BLOOD

N·M·BROWNE

BLOOMSBURY

LONDON BERLIN NEW YORK SYDNEY

Bloomsbury Publishing, London, Berlin, New York and Sydney

First published in Great Britain in July 2011 by Bloomsbury Publishing Plc
36 Soho Square, London, W1D 3QY

A CIP catalogue record for this book is available from the British Library

ISBN 978 1 4088 1255 6

Typeset by Hewer Text UK Ltd, Edinburgh
Printed in Great Britain by Clays Ltd, St Ives Plc, Bungay, Suffolk

1 3 5 7 9 10 8 6 4 2

www.bloomsbury.com

For Shirley Matthews and Laura Matthews Bailey,
my mother and my sister

CHAPTER ONE

Trista's Story

Cerys is dead. Her hot head lies in my lap, but already her skin cools in the damp air. We lie, her corpse and I, with the other slaves in the cold, dark curve of the roundhouse wall. She was my only friend.

She won't be the last to die this night. I know that death is coming for us all, riding on the snow-wind that howls louder than the wolves. I know it where it counts: in my bones and guts; death will be here soon.

I must move, but my back aches from the hard labour of the day and my legs are numb from the weight of Cerys. I can't feel anything. It is an effort to stroke her fine hair and trace the lines of her face with my fingers. I close her eyes and mutter a prayer for her soul.

'Shut your mouth, you stupid Brigante cow. I'm trying to sleep.' Elen's voice is a low snarl. She accompanies her words with a hard kick to my back. That blow was a mistake. I could kill her with my bare hands if I chose. I've kept my head down and my temper under control these last months for Cerys' sake. Now there is nothing to hold me back. Now no one can punish her for my faults. Cerys is free and so am I. The worst has happened and there is nothing else that I fear. Of course, I don't kill Elen. She's not my enemy, just another hard-used slave. This life has cut out the kindness from all of us. Anger is better than grief. Grief is useless. I should be grateful to Elen because anger gives me the strength to shuffle away from her on my knees, Cerys' slight body in my arms.

My cold breath mists the air. We are as far as we can be from the fire, the snoring Chief, his men, his kin, and the restless hounds. We are further still from the only door. I could have escaped before, but I was honourably taken in battle and then, when I realised there was no honour in enslavement to this Chief, Cerys needed me and I had to stay. She was little more than a child. I saved her from the Chief and the worst of the women's spite, but fever doesn't fight fair and I've no weapons against that. I cross her arms over her chest before she becomes too stiff to move. She was noble born and deserved better than this crumbling hole of a hall as a burial place. I have no grave gifts for her and that shames me, even as it gives me an idea.

The Chief and his men lie snoring in a stupor. There is

little food to be had in this the hungriest of times, but they have feasted on the last of the Falernian wine. They've been celebrating some trivial victory over strangers in the woods beyond the River Ddu. The gods have blessed me with their drunkenness.

Usually I keep my eyes from my captors. I'm warrior-trained and I've wanted them to forget it so I've skulked in the shadows for Cerys' sake. Humility has become a habit. I look at them now and though they bested us at Ragan's Field, I can't see how. I could kill them where they lie, vulnerable as babies, dribbling in their wine-soaked sleep as if death does not stalk them.

I crawl towards them across the stinking rushes. Bric, the Chief's finest hound, raises his head from his paws. He looks straight at me but his throaty growl is muted. The Chief is quick to anger and it is his dogs and his slaves who bear the brunt of it. I signal to the dog to lie back down. My father had a gift with animals and I have inherited a little of it. Bric obeys me. He is silent but watchful. The Chief's sword in its jewelled scabbard lies beside his overturned goblet, glinting gold in the firelight and not much more than a long arm's reach from where I kneel. I stretch my arm towards it. I can't quite touch it. I almost topple. Bric snarls and the Chief's eyes open. I hesitate. If the man chooses to attack, I will go down fighting. I can get to the sword before he can. My

3

blood thunders in my ears like the river in full flood. Somehow the Chief's bleary eyes focus only on the hound. He cuffs Bric hard so that the dog yelps and cowers from him, then the Chief grunts and settles back to sleep. Bric is between me and the blade. Slowly I list the names of all who died at Ragan's Field and only then, when I have calmed myself, do I move again. I pat Bric's skinny flanks and scratch behind his ears until he settles back down on his haunches and finally my fingers close round the precious sword. Still I dare not get to my feet but shuffle awkwardly back to Cerys, my long skirts tangling round my legs.

I ease the blade from the scabbard. The Chief, for all his slovenly ways, keeps its edge keen and the blade oiled. It is so good to hold a weapon again. I test its balance, grip its hilt in warrior fashion. Holding it, I am myself again. I can barely feel the blood flow through my fingers but I hold the sword against my jaw and slice cleanly with a steady hand. My hair is my only vanity. It has always been admired for its luxuriance and its reddish colour, the shade of old gold. I slice the plait just below my ear and when it falls away, I feel dizzy with sudden lightness. It is my only treasure and I arrange it like a torque around Cerys' neck – it is a kind of gold after all and the best I can do, even if it is less than she deserves. I don't risk rousing Elen again so my prayers are silent and hasty. Every nerve in my body is telling me it is time to go.

I am still too afraid to stand, but I fasten the sword belt around me. I've lost weight in the time I've been here and the elaborate decorated leather hangs too loosely from my hips. I hitch my skirts up above my knees and then I take Cerys' thick woollen cloak and brooch from her. I don't want to but I know she wouldn't begrudge it; the afterlife cannot be as grim and cold as this one.

I lift the sword so that it doesn't drag against the ground and crawl slowly past the sleeping men. The Chief's wife stirs and mutters in her sleep as I approach and one of the babies cries and is instantly put to the breast, but no one wakes for long enough to see me make my clumsy crawl for freedom with the Chief's best sword. Bric follows me with his eyes and I wish I could take him with me.

I don't get to my feet until I reach the door. I have to lean a little against the wall for balance. I'm not weak, just worn out with all that has happened and dizzy from lack of food. I wrap Cerys' cloak around my head and shoulders and secure it with her brooch. I unsheathe the sword, ready. I'm not ready, but I'd rather die of the cold than at the hands of the shining men who will take this hall before the night is over. I've seen them. Their metal tunics, splattered with blood, alive with reflected fire. Around them the flames of the blazing hall leap and flicker while the Chief and all his kin scream and die. I should warn them. I am a seeress and my visions are true. I falter for a moment. It is my duty to tell the Chief what I've seen, but duty and honour have only brought me here to this tumbledown hall, half starved as a winter hare, friendless and frozen. Besides, the Chief has a druid of his own.

It takes all my strength to lift the apron of leather that cuts out the draughts from the hall, to unbar the great door and push against it. Even the strange Parisi gods whose names I barely know are with me tonight, for someone has oiled the hinge and the great door swings open silently and suddenly I am engulfed by a blizzard. I can hear the hungry baying of the wolves and for an instant almost slink back into the lesser cold of the hall. It takes all my courage to step away from the shelter of the overhanging thatch. The watch are busy warming themselves at the brazier at the gate. I count the huddled shapes. They are all there, shirking their duty; they deserve what is to come.

Within five paces I am camouflaged by snow. It stings my face like the branding iron and blinds me. Luckily I know that it is fifty steps to the timber rampart of the fortress wall. I make them swiftly, praying that the watch are too distracted by their own discomfort to do their job. The sword bounces against my legs and my boots are worn so thin I feel every bump and stone of the ground, but worst of all I am afraid my heart will batter its way out of my chest it is banging so hard in my breast. When I get to the rampart, my legs give way and I collapse into the thick blanket of snow like a speared deer. It is so cold every gulping breath is full of knives. I have to wait until I stop shaking before I can begin to prod each wooden stake in the wall with my sheathed sword. Some will be rotten even in a well-run fort and this is not a well-run fort. It doesn't take me long to find a piece of wall that crumbles and then it is just a case of levering the timbers apart with my scabbard and bashing at it with the pommel of my sword. It is hard to hear anything in this wind and there is still no sign of the watch. I work at the timbers with my numb fingers until I can make a hole big enough for me. The wood, jagged as a broken tooth, scrapes the skin from my back but then I'm through.

I'd forgotten the sheerness of the slope beyond the rampart. I can't keep my feet. I have time to thank the triple-faced goddess for the thickness of the snow, then I slip and I'm tumbling, rolling, falling down and away from the place of my humiliation, bashed, almost broken . . . and free.

I can't see anything but whiteness. Ice stings my eyes and snow fills my mouth and ears. In the darkness I'm not sure which way is up and I'm thrashing around like a fish out of water. It's all right. I can breathe and I don't think anything is broken. I should run before the watch see what I've done to the wall, or before the flame-wielding enemy breaches the rampart. I struggle to get to my feet but pitch backwards into the wet snow because I am falling into that other darkness and another vision.

This time no one dies. I see only the face I've seen since I was a child. He is handsome as ever, naked and in chains. When I was little, before I was betrothed to Gwyn, I thought he was to be my husband. Now I don't know what to think. The man in my visions is older – twenty at least and built like a warrior. His dark eyes seem to bore into my soul. I shiver. My visions are rarely useful. They did not warn me that everyone I loved would die or that I would be enslaved. They show only pictures of places I've never been, men I've never seen and wolves. I've had too many visions of wolves. If I could be rid of my foreseeing, I would. Each episode leaves me shaking and disoriented. I melt some snow in my hands to quench my inevitable thirst. I've been sweating under my clothes and now my sweat will begin to cool and if I don't move, I'll die here of the cold. It would be a gentler death than many.

I struggle to my feet. The vision of the bright enemy was useful. I must act on that and flee this place. I brush myself down, check my sword and start to walk. I have twisted my ankle but it isn't serious and the pain sharpens my mind. It would be too easy to lie down in all this soft feathery whiteness, lie down and never wake. Perhaps the gods have spared me for a reason; I want to know what that might be.

CHAPTER TWO

Morcant's Story

'Get the fire going!' I do what I can to obey. These are the first words Lucius has spoken since the fight yesterday. He hasn't even called me 'a half-breed Keltic bastard'. I didn't think I'd miss that.

It wasn't my fault the Kelts attacked. It definitely wasn't my fault that the fat chieftain sliced through Julius' arm. Yes, I was slow drawing my sword but that was shock not cowardice. I'd like to explain, but that isn't how it works, not among soldiers.

Maybe Lucius has got us lost on purpose. He's a dirty, ill-tempered runt but a good scout. Here in this wood anything could happen to a callow new recruit and no questions would be asked of a veteran with a solid reputation. I check my short sword and my knife. I don't think I could take Lucius even in a fair fight and he's not known for fair fights.

The snow is deep here and it isn't easy to find wood that

will burn. I find a suitable spot and unload my gear. It's a relief to take off my pack. We had to let the others take the mule back to camp so we've had to carry everything we need. Without my kit I feel so light I could float. The snow has soaked through my scarf and cold water trickles down my back. At least my tinderbox is dry. I clear the snow from a flat patch of ground and use my axe to cut some branches, shaking away the snow. I hate these woods. My neck prickles as if we're observed. Ancient forests can be home to all kind of dangers, threats to the body and to the soul. This time I'll be ready. I'm not a coward.

The feeling of being watched grows as I build a fire and edge it with the few stones I can uncover in this bleached wilderness. It is worse now the wind has dropped and the snow no longer falls. The darkness is settling around us like soot on the snow and the silence and stillness lift the hairs on the nape of my neck. Somewhere a lone wolf howls and I shiver. My mother would say that someone walked on my grave, but she was an Armorican Kelt and steeped in superstition.

I fiddle around with tinder and flint but can't raise a spark. My hands are shaking with the cold and with this terrible sense that something bad is about to happen.

It is there when I look up. It can only be a wraith, a ghost creature – tall, white and hooded, staring at me with hollow

10

eyes. I cry out, but it sounds more like a pig's squeal than a man's voice and Lucius turns to me, startled. Even in the twilight I can see his lip curl in contempt.

I reach for my sword, but I know it will do no good against one of the shadow creatures of the deep forest. Lucius sees the creature and his reaction is swift and brutal. In three long strides his sword is against the creature's throat. Before he slices through it, the creature speaks. 'Please, I mean no harm.' The voice is low and unsteady and it speaks the language of the tribes. I didn't know that such dead things could speak in any tongue. Then the thing falls to the ground as if it were some mortal creature. It lands with a heavy thud on the snow as if it were flesh and blood. As I step closer I can smell the animal stink of the byre and the scent of woodsmoke mixed with the damp wool of its cloak.

'It's a man!'

'What else did you expect, you gelded son of a pox-ridden whore?'

'Don't kill him!'

'He's Keltic scum like you – what else should I do?'

The man's eyes flutter and open. His mouth works and then he speaks again.

'Please . . .'

'He might have information.' It is the first thing that comes into my head, but we do need intelligence about the

Keltic rebel leader Caratacus in particular and it is enough to make Lucius hesitate.

'Disarm him and tie him up. Then we'll see,' Lucius says.

I have rope in my pack. I fetch it, almost tripping over my sword in my haste. Under Lucius' unforgiving gaze I haul the man roughly to his feet. We stand eye to eye and I'm the tallest in the legion. The darkness shadows his face but something about his presence bothers me. 'Do you have a weapon?'

He raises his arms so that his cloak falls back and even in the dusk I can see the scabs over a slave brand. I pat him down. He wears a sword belt that is very fine and obviously stolen. I don't think his bulky shawl hides another weapon, but I have been told to be thorough in all my duties as a soldier. I slide my hands under the cloak to check that he doesn't carry a hidden knife. I don't find another weapon, but I find myself blushing.

'I mean no harm.' The low voice is sullen now. Not a wraith then but a thief, and more – a woman. I don't need to share that information with Lucius. I wouldn't trust him with a woman. I take the sword and on impulse fasten the sword belt around my own waist. The blade sits more comfortably against my hip than the short Roman gladius I carry.

'What do you think you're doing with that, you little bastard Brit? I'll have the spoils,' Lucius says, his harsh soldier's Latin an offence against the gods of this place.

'Of course,' I say hastily, 'I'm just wearing it while I tie him up.'

Lucius snorts but leaves me to it, busying himself with sorting through his pack.

'Before you tie me, let me help light your fire.' She speaks in little more than a whisper. It's cold and the wood is wet. 'There is a trick I know that will save you time.' Did she see me fail before? 'It will only take a moment.' I believe her. Besides, I have the sword and, while I'm not the best of fighters, I couldn't be bested by a woman. I place myself between her and Lucius' line of sight. I have my gladius out and I will stab her if she makes a threatening move. She squats by the fire, as all tribespeople do. As I do. She waves away my offer of my tinderbox and does something with her hands that I can't see. The light is fading fast. She didn't lie – in moments the fire catches and the damp wood begins to burn. It is quite a trick.

When she stands up, she holds out her hands for me to tie them. Now I know she is a woman it is impossible to see her as anything else. The face the firelight shows is young and gaunt but not unattractive. Her wrists are bony.

I let her sit by the fire and her shawl slips from her head to reveal raggedly cut hair the colour of Keltic gold.

'I am Morcant,' I say, 'and my comrade is Lucius.'

'He is not your master?'

'No. We are both soldiers of Legio IX.'

She doesn't look as though she believes me, though she nods politely. My mother always said that it is not wise to give away your name, but I'm Roman now and have no truck with such views. The woman shares my mother's opinion: she does not give her name.

I unpack the rest of my kit, finding my cook pot and food. It's just travelling rations – bread, cheese and beans to cook up, but she can't hide the hunger in her eyes as she watches me.

I give her some bread and she nibbles it, as if to make it last.

'When did you last eat?'

She shrugs. 'I've been walking since before dawn – I ate some broth yesterday.' Lucius turns and sees me give the woman a piece of cheese. She needs it more than I do.

'Mithras' balls – what are you doing wasting rations on Brit shit?' He tries to grab the bread from the woman's hand and then when his hand touches hers he snatches his back as if stung.

'What the . . .'

'Tell him not to be afraid. I'm a seeress, that is all, and our touch can bring on a sharing.' I don't know what she means. The druid of my mother's people never mentioned such a thing, but then he was old and ignorant as muck. Lucius is

14

looking murderous. Before I can translate her words she speaks again.

'Tell him I can see his wife with a dark-haired baby at her breast. She is sick, dying I think, but the baby is strong as is the little boy who stands by her bed. The boy will live.'

I don't want to translate this but I do. I don't sheathe my gladius though, just in case Lucius tries to kill her. I am a soldier of Rome now and of course I will do my duty, but I won't let Lucius kill an unarmed woman at any hearth of mine.

Lucius turns silent when I translate her words. He stares at the fire as if lost. I think it might be all right and then he roars, 'No! You lying piece of Keltic scum.' His sword is out and he is about to gut her with it. His response is not unexpected, but mine is. I drop my shoulder and tackle him, which is stupid. Luckily, he is so surprised he doesn't slice me as he ought to do. He lands hard on the snow with me on top of him. He is a veteran though, and he doesn't let go of his gladius. I get to my feet in a flurry of snow. He is winded, which gives me time to plant myself in front of the woman as if to protect her. She's nothing to me, but I don't trust Lucius to stop at killing her. I'll be next.

'What by Mithras' cock are you doing?' He is gasping for air.

'We haven't questioned him yet. You know we had orders

to question any captured natives about Caratacus.' I let Lucius get to his feet, which is a mistake because he's coming for me now. The woman is standing too, a looming presence behind me. She takes advantage of my confusion to wrest the longsword from my belt. She is quick as a snake or a warrior. Now I'm caught between the two of them. It happens quickly. Lucius charges me and I am too slow to use my gladius. Instead, on instinct, I put out my foot. It is a cheap trick that should not have worked on an old and canny veteran, but it does. Lucius trips and falls headlong into the fire. It was such a small blaze his bulk should have extinguished it with little damage; instead, from nowhere huge flames leap, wild and out of control. He screams and the fire consumes him. It is too hot for me to try to save him. The heat burns my face and singes my eyebrows. The woman cries out and both of us step back from the inferno – we have no choice. The smell is terrible. Lucius' cry is like nothing I've ever heard. It is swiftly over and then the fire shrinks back almost to nothing and Lucius is a charred and blackened corpse.

I am trembling and I stammer when I finally manage to speak.

'W-what in Lugh's name h-h-happened?'

'You killed him.' The woman's tone is accusing but her voice quavers too. She seems as shaken as I am.

'Not me. You killed him with your fire.'

She shakes her head. We are both bearing unsheathed weapons. She holds the longsword like a warrior; I hold my gladius like a fool. I'm not about to kill her; I don't know if she plans on killing me.

'How did you do it?'

She shakes her head. 'I didn't. *You* tripped him!' She sounds scornful and then adds more softly, 'Perhaps the gods of this place do not like foreigners.' We both look around. The wood beyond the glow of the killing fire is dark and sinister.

I unbuckle her sword belt clumsily and hand it back to her. Keltic women are not like Romans. I know that, in spite of the slave brand, she is of the warrior caste. I was wrong before – I could be bested by such a woman. She only hesitates for a moment before taking the belt. She watches me and sheathes her sword as I put away my gladius. The tension between us eases a little.

'Do you often kill your own in your Legio IX?' She pronounces the foreign words awkwardly, but that does nothing to dull the sharpness of her words. What small control I had of this situation is slipping away. I didn't kill Lucius. It was an accident, that is all. I imagine explaining that to our Decanus, Marcellus, and then up the chain of command to our Praefectus Castrorum – a grizzled veteran of uncertain temper who served with Lucius in Gaul. I can see my father's

17

dream of my glorious army career turn to ash along with Lucius' corpse. It is never going to happen now. I don't think I dare return to our fort, even assuming I could find my way. Julius thinks I let him down in our earlier encounter with the Kelts and how can I account for Lucius' death? I speak the tribal tongues – maybe I could disguise myself as a local Kelt and make my way to my mother's people in Armorica? All this passes through my head in the space between the woman's pointed question and my response.

'I didn't kill him and it's not my Legio IX,' I say and I know that I'm not going back.

Smoke is still rising from Lucius' body.

'I have to bury him,' I say.

'The ground is frozen solid, you'd be better building a cairn.' She's right of course, but I get out my spade anyway and then I hear the wolves howl.

CHAPTER THREE

Trista's Story

Morcant freezes when the wolves howl. I don't blame him. They seem so much closer here. Should I keep walking? I don't want to run into wolves; I don't know where I'm going, my legs are trembling from weakness, and it is good to have company. This man is kind. He gave me food. It is a long time since anyone has given me anything besides a beating and I know I could take him in a fight with one arm tied behind my back and both eyes closed. Strange, he is tall and well-built and ought to have what it takes to make a warrior.

Instead of moving on I find myself helping him bury the corpse of his comrade. We have to cool him down with snow before we can move him.

'Help me take off his shirt,' I say.

'What?'

Even in the firelight I can see that Lucius' mail shirt is a masterful piece of work, linked chains of metal that would protect me like a blessing from the mother. I recognise it. The enemies of my vision wore such shirts, and other shinier things. Wearing one of them would be like wearing a shield, leaving both arms free for fighting.

'I want his shirt, and his helmet too. If I come across any more of you Romans, I want what you have.'

He helps me reluctantly. He's very fastidious for a soldier. I doubt he's seen action yet; I'm not sure he'd survive. It is a grisly job and even I avert my eyes from Lucius' ruined, melted face.

The ground is like iron and so we do a poor job, merely heaping snow and stones over his body. I say prayers to Lugh and the triple-faced one and Morcant mumbles something about Mithras. I'm glad to get back to the fire. The night is full of unseen things, creatures of the forest watching us, waiting for us beyond the small circle of light we have made with our fire and unlikely companionship.

'Here, you might as well have this – he doesn't need it now.'

He gives me Lucius' pack full of spare clothes, a goatskin canteen of water, and food. I don't eat right away but drink deeply of the water then dress myself in Lucius' tunic and Keltic trews. They are too short of course but much more use to me than my long women's skirts. I clean off Lucius' mail shirt too and Morcant watches me struggling into it, while he heats beans over the fire. I feel better for the extra clothes. If I meet the shining men of my vision, it will now be on more equal terms.

The food is better still. So hot it burns my mouth but I don't care.

'How long have you been a soldier?' He has offered me hospitality of sorts and I am bound by old rules to make myself pleasant in the acceptance of it.

He fingers a new-looking tattoo on his hand – a wolf. I am a little startled by that. I think of the wolf as my own symbol, for my many visions of wolves.

'I've been training since the summer.'

'But you're of the tribes?' He has that look about him. He reminds me a little of Gwyn, though his features are finer, his eyes greyer and his expression sweeter. In fact he looks nothing like him – it is just that he is handsome. It is not a thought I should be having in the middle of this wilderness when I am on the run from his own compatriots.

'My mother was a slave from Armorica, my father a Roman, an army veteran from Rome itself. He has no other children so he acknowledged me as his heir. I'm a citizen.'

'Will you go back to your . . .' I search for the right word. 'Your fighting tribe?'

'My legion? No. I don't think so. They will blame me for Lucius' death.' He scrapes the pot of beans and gives me the last of it. I'm too hungry not to accept.

'I don't think the life is for me anyway – it feels all wrong.'

I don't answer. There is something wrong about him. I don't know what it is, but something niggles in my marrow, in my seer's guts.

'What about you?' He asks the question gently. A seeress is bound to truth but I don't think an escaped slave is bound by anything.

'I was a warrior once, of one of the Brigante clans. I was captured in battle by the Parisi. I escaped.'

'You said you were a seeress?' Is he mocking me?

'It's a gift. I'm not initiated.' He waits for me to go on and for some inexplicable reason I do. 'My father was sent to Mona to study with the druids as a boy. He swore that no child of his would ever be druid trained.' He raises his eyebrows at that, as well he might. My father gave up the honour and power of a druid for a life training horses and dogs. He counted it a good bargain too. It was fortunate for us children that he was born of warrior stock, with generous sisters, or we would have had nothing.

'Ah well, we all live at the whim of our fathers.' His smile takes the sting from his words but he sounds sad. No doubt he is a disappointment to his own father and I can see why. 'Where are you headed?'

The change of subject is abrupt but welcome. I don't want to talk about the past.

22

I shrug. 'Away from your army, back to Brigante lands. I don't know. You?'

'Armorica. Away from the army too.'

It is on the tip of my tongue to ask him if we should travel together when another wolf's cry echoes around us. By Lugh, they are very close now. My hand finds the hilt of my sword.

'We should sleep in turns,' he says quickly, 'to watch the fire and keep the wolves at bay.'

I nod. I have always feared that my visions of wolves are a sign that they will be the harbinger of my death, but I don't say that.

I get up to put more wood on the fire. Morcant takes it from me and then our hands touch. He pulls his hand sharply away but I cry out.

'No!'

I am backing away from him now, grabbing Lucius' shield and long spear as I go.

'What is it?' He looks around wildly as if to see what has frightened me. Surely he must know?

'You!'

'What are you talking about?'

'You are a shape-changer, a wolfman, a werewolf!'

My back is to the tree now. He walks towards me, laughing nervously.

'What are you talking about? That's just Keltic super-stition. There's no such thing.'

He seems utterly in earnest. He truly does not know what he is. His eyes flash yellow in the fire's glow and I reach for my sword.

CHAPTER FOUR

Trista's Story

Morcant puts his hands up as if in surrender. His hands are large and look strong.

'You don't need to use your sword, warrior-seeress lady. I don't wish to insult your gifts, but you're mistaken. Come back to the fire.'

I'm not mistaken. Now that I've seen his nature I cannot unsee it. If I half close my eyes, I can see the faint shadow of a sleeping wolf that surrounds him. Still, I hesitate. The safety of the fire draws me. There are eldritch things beyond it, unseen creatures of unknown intent. It is hard to believe that this ungainly man could be much of a threat to me. I am armed, after all. Morcant's smile is wide, innocent, but his eyes glint with an animal light, cold as the Chief's metal mirror. I stay where I am. He shrugs. His shoulders are broad, his chest deep. I must not let his gentle manner beguile me. He could be a powerful man.

'You shouldn't travel alone,' he says, but his words are slurred. He stretches, yawns, then does what I least expect. He drops to all fours by the fire, like a child playing at being a hound. I tighten my grip on Lucius' spear. What is he doing? He seems to have forgotten that he is observed. He stretches his long back, and then extends his neck as if for an executioner's blade. His expression is curiously dreamy. He sighs gently with – what? Relief? Contentment? I have no idea. He shudders and closes his eyes. For the first time I see the shadow wolf open his. The beast's eyes are startling, alert, hard, everything that Morcant's aren't. Those eyes are a shock. The shadow wolf is a living creature, real as I am.

It is hard to make sense of what happens next. The man's outline blurs as if I am seeing it through tear-filled eyes. I want to rub my eyes but dare not let go of my weapon. Morcant's very body fades, the shape and colour of him leaching away to become a ghostly silver. At the same instant the half-seen shadow wolf becomes clearer as if finally coming into focus. No. It is more than that. He is not just coming into focus, he is becoming flesh and blood. Hands become paws, pale human skin becomes dark, bestial fur, Morcant's fine nose and chin coarsen and thicken to become an animal muzzle. The man has become a wolf in front of my eyes. There's no cracking of bones nor straining of tendons, just this noiseless swapping of forms. How can this be possible? My guts twist at the strangeness of it. Should I run? I fear the wolf would outpace me for this isn't any ordinary wolf; just as Morcant is big for a man, this creature is huge for a wolf. He is still draped in Morcant's clothes.

He turns his attention and razor teeth to escaping from the restriction of mail shirt and sword belt. He growls his displeasure – a low, terrifying sound at the back of his throat. Now might be the time to run, but I can't make my legs move. I've never seen anything like this and it fascinates me as much as it terrifies me. I can see the spectral form of Morcant the man around this wild creature: he is sleeping as peacefully as a child. I know little of shapeshifters but I am certain that the man should always be master of the beast. The druids, who practise such magics, gain the attributes of animals but lose none of their own power. Here there is no doubt as to which creature is in charge and this creature fixes me with its predator's eyes. There is no trace of Morcant in them, no softness, no human intelligence, nothing, in fact, but hunger.

I adjust my grip on Lucius' spear. The weight of it is different from the Keltic type. It has a long metal shaft attached to a wooden pole and lacks the charms and druid blessings which give ours a greater potency. I'll have one chance to hit the beast if he pounces and I cannot miss. If Morcant dies along with the wolf, that is not my fault. I will not hesitate for sentiment's sake: I will live.

The wolf's eyes meet mine and I don't look away. He looks at the spear and does not back down. He growls.

I can't afford to be afraid. If I allow my hand to tremble when I throw, I will not throw true. I survived the battle of Ragan's Field because I fought my fear. My heart beats quickly six or seven times and then I hear a wolf howl. It is close by, closer even than before. The effect on the wolf is instant: he raises his head to the bright moon and bays a response. The sound sends shivers down my spine. Somehow the wolf's cry sounds anguished, desolate, the loneliest cry I've ever heard. Perhaps there is an answering yowl that I cannot hear because it seems that he has forgotten all about me and bounds off after the wolf pack. The man, Morcant, is gone with him.

I can't move for several more heartbeats, but stand clutching my spear. My knuckles turn white with the needless pressure. I've lost my knack of overcoming fear.

I stagger back to the fire and sit there in shock. I thought I wouldn't mind dying now I've lost so much. I was wrong.

It takes a while to get my racing thoughts in order. I keep returning to what I've just seen, trying to picture exactly what happened. I shake my head hard as if that will shake away the memory. I have to forget about the mystery I've seen enacted and find a way to survive the rest of the night. The wolf will return. It is likely he will return with other wolves. There's little to eat even for hunters at this time of year and I am sitting not ten paces from a corpse. The stink of it, too faint yet for human noses, will draw the wolves here like men to mead.

I run through several wild ideas before settling on my plan. First I clear away some of the snow and heavy stones from Lucius' pyre. I don't like doing it, because I was brought up to honour the dead. I pray to the gods that Lucius' shade might forgive me, but all things are permitted to the desperate. Then I return to the fire and, using the flat of Lucius' short sword, extract some hot coals from the glowing heart of it and place them in Lucius' copper, loop-handled cook pot. The heat turns the blade as black as my chain mail. I don't intend to die of the cold so I wrap my newly made firepot in Morcant's tunic and secure the bundle to my belt by the tunic's arms. I enfold myself in Morcant's cloak as well as my own, stuff all the food still remaining in Lucius' pack, take his canteen and head for the trees. I don't want to stray far from the camp, the extra weapons and the fire, but if I stay on the ground I'm easy meat. I can't fight a pack of wolves on my own, not in my weakened, exhausted state. I have to sleep, rest, survive and then decide what to do next.

It is years since I climbed a tree – once I was betrothed it was deemed unseemly. Before that I spent half my girlhood shinning up the ancient oaks in our woodland. I hope I haven't forgotten how.

The tree nearest the fire isn't an oak but a fir with little in the way of lower branches. I've thought of that. This is a good moment to remind myself of how to throw a spear.

My first attempt is pathetic, incompetently thrown and poorly aimed. I hear the ghost of Gwyn mocking my frailty with his characteristic bitter wit. I grit my teeth and try again, this time with Morcant's spear. The spear hits the tree trunk squarely and well. I run to check. The spear is deeply embedded in the bark to the depth of half my hand's span. That will have to do. I daren't risk another attempt. I hurl Lucius' pack up into the lower branches of the tree. It's bulky and an awkward shape. It takes me several weary throws before it catches in the branches. It doesn't look secure, but it's too late to do anything about that. I grab the first spear from where it fell uselessly into the snowy ground and tuck it under my arm. I tighten the cloaks around me and make sure my sword is secure. Now comes the test. I use the spear buried in the trunk to give me a leg-up. It buckles, though I'm lighter than I was. I don't give it a chance to break but haul myself with all my strength up into the tree. I am out of practice but my body remembers what to do. At least I've gained in strength and reach what I've lost in agility. I can still do it. I make it to the safety of the largest branch with no time at all to spare. When I look down, I can see dark shapes prowling and snuffling at the tree's roots. The wolves are here.

CHAPTER FIVE

Trista's Story

Thank Lugh, the horned one and the mother, but natural wolves don't climb. I'm less sure about the werewolf. I don't breathe for a bit, then I realise that I can't hold my breath all night. The wolves know I'm here – they just can't get to me. It feels like a long time before they drift away one by one, drawn by the scent of easier prey, the carrion that was once Lucius. I can hear them digging at the fresh snow, uncovering what Morcant and I had so recently buried. I block my ears to the sounds that follow.

There is one gift common to both a warrior and a slave and that is the ability to grab sleep whenever and wherever you can – no matter how precarious the situation. It is a gift I've perfected over long years. I hang my firepot on a branch and feed it all the dry pine needles that I can. I then arrange my cloaks to give me maximum protection against the cold and drift off.

It's cramp that wakes me. I've no idea how long I've slept but I have to stretch out my leg. I'm stiff, chilled to the bone and in some pain. I try to massage out the knotty muscles with numb hands and somehow I knock over the firepot so that it falls down through the interlaced branches below me, bouncing off them noisily as it goes. It lands with a noticeable thud and an avalanche of snow. I might just as well have called out to the wolves to come and get me. Two of them are there in a heartbeat, prowling around the tree and whimpering. I had hoped they would be too well fed by now to bother me. It looks like I'll have to try the second part of my survival plan, once I've rid myself of the cramp anyway. I keep a close lookout and squint to see beyond this tree to the camp. I think the other wolves may have gone. There are just these two to deal with. It is hard to tell from this distance but I think one of them might be Morcant.

I use the end of the spear to cut a strip of fabric from the bottom of Morcant's cloak and I bind it around the long metal shaft and tip. One spear; two wolves. I'll have to kill the one and scare away the other. I will not be able to do either job from my present position. I can't stay here much longer in any case, unless I want to die of cold. I have to rub my hands together to warm them and then tuck them under my armpits. Neither works – they are still stiff and it hurts to move my fingers. I wait until I can see a dark shape under the tree and then throw my borrowed pack down. The wolf leaps back with a yelp as I miss its head by less than a hand span. Pity. Now for the difficult part. I begin to climb back down and when I reach the lowest branch I leave the safety of the tree's canopy and wrap my legs around the tree trunk and try to hold myself steady. These months of slavery have weakened me. It is very uncomfortable but I need to be below the pine-covered branches in order to have the space to attack. I will have to be quick. I try to find the fire inside me, the spark of flame that I can sometimes will into being. It is hard to concentrate when I am so worried that I'm going to fall straight down into the waiting jaws of the wolves a spear's length below me. I can see them both now. I should have a clear shot. I almost lose my balance getting the spear into position and then I breathe in slowly and breathe out flame. Only nothing happens. Oh, may the gods of my tribe not desert me now! I shut my eyes and steady myself as if for battle. There. I breathe in and out and this time flame blooms along the fabric wound round the spear shaft. I take aim.

One of the wolves reacts immediately to the sound and scent of fire and begins to run deeper into the forest. The sky is lightening, dawn is not long away, and I can see the beast quite well. I time the throw as I've been trained, estimating the wolf's speed. I count to myself. My muscles are burning with the unfamiliar strain of keeping me securely wrapped round the tree. I can't hold much longer. I let the spear fly. It is not my best shot. It misses the neck and spine of the running wolf, only grazing its flank. The creature yelps and disappears from view. I've not killed it nor have I frightened the other. Gwyn would have had something to say about that.

I can't see the second wolf, the wolf that might be Morcant. Perhaps I've been luckier than I deserve and I have scared him away? Either way, I am too cold to stay where I am. I let myself slide down the trunk, scraping the inside of my thighs. The second my feet hit the ground my sword is out. I pull the spear out of the trunk using all my remaining strength and try to make sense of the tracks around the tree.

I move as stealthily as my stiff joints allow until I see one set of wolf prints change into the distinctive form of a man's bare foot. Morcant must have transformed back! I feel a surge of something – relief? Hard to know. Maybe it is hope. Maybe I will survive the night.

I am alert for any sign that the wolf pack might lurk here still but I think they've gone. It is getting lighter all the time. The sun is not yet fully up and everything is bleached grey, grainy and unreal. The prone, naked figure of Morcant the man looks waxy. Is he alive? His skin is tinged with blue, but his chest rises and falls quite regularly. He does not stir as I cover him with his own cloak and turn my attention to restarting the fire. I keep my spear within reach in case he wakes and attacks but I'm not expecting that. The shadow of the wolf still surrounds him but the wolf sleeps as heavily as the man.

It takes a while for me to warm up and all the time I watch the sleeping man. Who knows what this transformation will have done to him? I notice the very moment when his eyelids flicker and his eyes open. His eyes in daylight are a greenish grey with flecks of a wolfish yellow. Their owner looks confused. He tries to speak but nothing comes out of his mouth and I see the panic in his face. He coughs and puts one grimy hand to his head to push away his thick, dark hair.

'What happened?' His voice is hoarse as if he had been shouting all night. His nails are black half-moons of muck and his hands are streaked with blood. 'I had a strange dream . . .'

I wait.

'Do you know . . . I mean . . . how?' He indicates his nakedness. I don't reply.

He doesn't appear hostile. He has a lost look in his eyes and I struggle to see him as a potential enemy. He shivers and I dig in his bag for his remaining clothes. 'You need to dress,' I say and he twists away from me modestly. I'm used to the company of men and don't need such consideration. His body is smeared with dirt and dried blood and raked with claw marks. It doesn't look like he had an easy night.

I help him with his boots and with the fastenings of his belt: I am not half-witted enough to strap on his sword. His hands and fingers are clumsy, as if he has forgotten how to use them. His skin is cold as stone. I tend him as I tended the sick back at home, as I tended Cerys. He lets me help him with such child-like trust that I wonder if his mind has been damaged by his transformation.

I boil snow over the now blazing fire and make a meal from the last of Morcant's food supplies – barley, beans and cheese. After my time at the Chief's fort it is a feast. Morcant eats ravenously. Whatever else happened, I don't think he feasted with the wolves last night and I'm relieved that he didn't eat Lucius' corpse. The blood on his hands is probably his own.

'You need to remember what happened.' I try to speak gently.

'I've not been drinking?'

'Only water from your canteen.'

I leave him to his disjointed thoughts. His confusion is no concern of mine.

Now that the sun is up, I know I should get moving but it is so good to rest in front of this fire. I let my mind drift, planning where to go next, how to find food. The only sound is the crackling of the fire, the spitting of the damp wood. At last he speaks.

'I remember running and some kind of fight.'

'You were a wolf, Morcant,' I say. 'A wild beast.'

He shakes his head. Even now he doesn't believe it. There is a rustle in the bushes and I have my sword out and I'm on my feet. Morcant is slower to react. That decides it. Tempting though it would be to travel with a companion, Morcant is too much of a risk – either wild predator or helpless fool. I check the undergrowth but see nothing untoward. It is time to go.

I pack up Lucius' gear, his cook pot, shield and spear. I leave his spade, axe and various other items for which I have no use or which weigh too much. I bow towards the hearth to thank the goddess and towards the tree that sheltered me through the long night. 'I thank you for the blessing of your fire and the shared food,' I say.

He's watching me with wide eyes. I can't see him living long like this but he's not my responsibility. I am free.

'Thanks for the food. May the gods look favourably on your journey,' I say. In the cool morning light I can see the wolf stirring. I turn my back on both of them and start walking. The spear is useful as a walking stick over the treacherous, uneven ground and, while the shield and armour are cumbersome, I leave Morcant's company better equipped than I arrived.

I don't know where Morcant's Legio IX might be camped, but they cannot be far away and I am afraid I've stayed here too long. I head north because I know the Brigante lands lie to the North of the Parisi. But that is all I know.

I haven't gone more than ten paces when it happens again – the dizziness and weakness. I hope Morcant doesn't see me sit down abruptly so that I don't fall. When the vision comes, it is sharp as a stab wound in my mind – I am in the Chief's hall as the legion comes. Elen and the rest of them are screaming. Swords slash through flesh and bone and the ground is slick with the blood of the slaughter. I choke and cough as the thick black smoke of the hall's fire catches in my throat, my eyes stream, nausea grips me.

My vision clears and I'm back in the snow-covered grove. I wipe snow across my face to revive me. I don't know if this massacre has happened or is yet to come but I've got to get further away. The hall and all this horror are still too near.

'Hey! Hold on! Are you all right?' Morcant's voice is different, strong, 'You can't travel alone!'

Of course I can travel alone. I turn back to answer him and see that the wolf wraith is fully awake now and restless. The wolf returns my look and does not look away, but sniffs the air, ready to move on. The man is already putting out the fire and gathering up his kit. 'Are you hurt?'

His movements are swift, neat, and in moments he is with me and helping me to my feet. His arm is strong; he almost lifts me from the ground.

'I'm fine,' I say, irritated. 'We'd both be better off travelling alone.' I know my voice trembles with weakness because it always does after a vision, but that doesn't mean I'm weak. I'll be stronger in a moment.

'No. It's much safer if we travel together – we can sleep in turns.' I don't argue. I haven't yet got the strength. Besides, it is the wolf I hear in Morcant's voice – assured, with the promise of violence. Short of putting a spear through Morcant's guts, I don't think there's much I can do. Could I have chosen a worse travelling companion? It is hard to imagine one.

I must still be befuddled by my vision, because when I allow him to help me it is with a lighter heart than I've had in a long time.

CHAPTER SIX

Morcant's Story

The female is sick, she smells wrong. Perhaps I am sick too and that's why I can't remember last night. There are shadows: smells, sounds that I can almost recall – fever dreams, nothing more. I'll be fine if I keep moving away from this forest, away from this country. The woman recovers quickly and strides ahead. I focus on following her long, straight back. I could almost imagine she were Lucius leading the way if she were not so tall. I know everything is not as it was yesterday; my churning guts and the chill in the marrow of my bones tell me that everything is different.

When the sun is high, we stop for a drink of water. It's still cold but the sun is bright and the snow is beginning to thaw. At least our trail of footprints in the snow will melt.

'We need to find something to eat.' She doesn't answer.

'Do you remember what happened yet?' I shake my head. She gives me a look that is close to contempt.

'You need to try harder,' she says and her eyes are very cold.

We walk and then walk some more. Even the army is not so hard a taskmaster as this woman. We leave the forest behind and come to an area of tilled ground. The woman stops, then 'By Lugh, no,' she whispers and what little I can see of her flesh is corpse white.

'What is it?'

'These are the Chief's fields. I've brought us back full circle. This is the place I ran from.'

The stench of fire is in the air: ash, charcoal, burned flesh.

'Shall we turn round?'

'No. The gods have brought me here for a reason, I must see what they want me to see.' Her voice is flat and lifeless. She already knows what she will see and so do I. We walk on.

It's not long before we see the ruins of a hill fort rising before us, the ramparts blackened and broken like old men's teeth. A pall of smoke still hangs overhead like a funeral cloak, like vulture's wings. I don't want to go any closer.

She hesitates and I can smell her fear. The smoke tells its own tale. I move to stand beside her.

'No one could survive this,' she says bleakly, but I know she is wrong. I can smell fresh blood – someone is still breathing, still bleeding. I don't argue with her. I stride ahead,

41

following the scent trail. She doesn't question me and I hear her behind me. I admire her courage.

I climb the steep slope of the hill. The stench of death is stronger here, mixed with the smoke that catches in my throat, in my eyes, my nose. It is on my tongue so that it is all I can taste. The white snow is black with ash. The wooden palisade still smoulders, burned to charcoal – it crumbles under my hands. This place is eerily silent. All the birds have flown away and no dogs bark a warning at our presence. They died here too. I can smell them.

I can see the ruin of the hall. They burn well, these round-houses; thatch catches so easily. There isn't much left within the smouldering remains. I guess that those unfortunate enough to be trapped inside huddled together for protection and were slaughtered where they stood. The corpses are all heaped to one side of the building. The ground is littered with shards of pottery and blackened iron. Anything of value has been stripped from the dead and taken. Still the scent of life draws me. I step over blackened timber. My hobnail boots crunch on ash and cinders. The dead are not long cold but already the decay has begun.

I find her at last, crouched in the shelter of the partially collapsed wall, all but hidden by the carrion. She is so stained with grime and soot that if I'd been depending on my eyes I would have missed her. She looks like a pile of rags. She opens her eyes at my approach and I see the fear in them.

'I've not come to harm you,' I say quickly in my mother's tongue. I offer her my canteen. I can see burns on her hands and death in her eyes so I hold it to her lips and tilt it gently so that she can drink.

My female companion is beside me. I glance up. She has removed both her helmet and her shawl to expose her face. Her eyes are moist but whether from the smoke or from grief I can't say.

'Elen?'

'Come to see your handiwork, bitch?' The burned woman's voice is dry and raw, the sound a parched rock might make if it could speak. She tries to spit in our direction but her mouth is too try and her lips scorched.

'This is not of my doing.' I hear anguish in my companion's voice

'Tell that to the Chief – he found your witchcraft just before your men came and did this.' She coughs – a ghastly, racking sound.

'The Chief survived?' The seeress sounds incredulous. I can't blame her. My army are good at bringing death and we rarely leave witnesses. 'He cursed you, Trista, and he'll get you!'

Elen tries to point a fire-ravaged, blistered finger at us, but the effort is too much. She grimaces with pain.

'I did no witchcraft!'

Elen is finding it harder and harder to breathe, let alone speak. I offer her more water. She moves her head away.

'Hair,' she says. I don't know what she means. The seeress seems to understand.

'Cerys died – of the fever that night, before I left. That was my offering, my gift to her for the next life. I'd nothing else.' She sounds desperate to explain; it's pointless – the woman, Elen, has already gone.

'She's dead, Trista.' At least now I know her name.

'I know.' She walks away from me, examining the ruin of her home.

I close the dead woman's eyes. There is nothing else we can do for her. I give Trista a moment to recover herself.

'What do you want to do?' I try to speak gently. I need not have bothered, Trista's eyes when she turns to look at me are cold, as hard as flint and quite dry.

'I need to get away from here. The Chief is still alive and blaming me for this.' She waves her arm to encompass the devastation. 'If I had the power to do this, I wouldn't have waited so long.' I am taken aback by her bitterness until I remember her slave brand. This was not her home but her prison. I don't suggest we stay and bury the corpses and neither does she.

She spends a few minutes digging around in the ash and

returns with a small sack of grain and some turnips. 'There was a store below the ground, but there's not much left.' We share what there is between us to make it easy to carry.

'You take the lead,' she says to my surprise, 'I have done a poor job. I want to go north, away from here, towards Brigantia, and I want to stay clear of your Legio IX. They can't be too far away and if this is their work they are best avoided.'

I nod. I couldn't agree more. Legio IX, my old legion, is indeed to be avoided.

CHAPTER SEVEN

Trista's Story

I can't forget Elen's face. I didn't like her – she was sour and vindictive – but it still galls me that she blamed me for what happened. The gods are playing some bitter game of their own in letting the Chief live. He is as unforgiving a bastard as ever drew breath and a vicious, ugly fighter. He is not an enemy I would ever have chosen. He must have found Cerys' body before the legion arrived. I couldn't find her among the dead, though I didn't look too hard.

The shadow wolf wrinkles his nose at the stench and Morcant is shocked to paleness but doesn't vomit or otherwise disgrace himself. We don't linger and to my relief Morcant doesn't ask me any questions. I ask enough of myself. Should I have warned them? Will the Chief enact the gods' revenge for my failure as a seeress?

We walk for a long time. Melting snow drips from every branch and the hard ground has turned to slush. My feet are sodden and the mail shirt weighs me down, but I'm not going to ask Morcant to stop. He seems as anxious as I am to put distance between us and the slaughter at the hall. Finally, he comes to a halt at a sheltered, defensible place between the wood and the river. It's a good choice.

'This looks a safe enough place to stop. We can refill our canteens, build a fire and dry out.' I nod. There's a risk that if I sit down I will never get up again.

There is very little dry wood here but we find what we can. I don't wait for Morcant to pull out his tinderbox, but start the fire immediately in my own way. He looks startled but I'm too tired to care. A man who turns into a wolf has little cause to be surprised by my gifts. I boil up the grain on the fire while he peels and slices the turnip. He finds a small twist of salt in the bottom of his pack that helps to make the meal more palatable. Not that the taste matters. I am hungry enough to eat my own shoe leather; it's doing my feet little good.

The sky is a pale winter blue streaked with downy cloud and the sunlight is wan but warming. My belly is full and my feet are thawing. I begin to relax until I see the wolf wraith's alert stance. He has sensed something, I know it.

'What's wrong?' Morcant asks. He is quick to put a hand to his own weapon.

'You should know. Your wolf is awake and sensing danger.'

47

Morcant's eyes narrow and he scowls. 'Very funny. Did you hear something?'

For a moment I thought I did. The wolf cocks his head on one side. Morcant is about to speak, but I silence him. I thought I heard voices.

'You should pay more attention to the wolf. He's sharper than you are.'

'Why do you keep talking about a wolf?' He is obviously irritated. He flares his nostrils and cocks his own head to one side as if aping the wolf. 'I think I can smell horses – a way off.'

'And that's because you're a shapeshifter, Morcant, a wolfman. Last night you transformed and joined a pack of wild wolves . . . That's what you don't remember.' I am whispering now, but loudly.

The wolf glowers, transparent as a raindrop in the sunlight but clear enough to me. I think he is growling and I see a flicker of the same fury in Morcant's yellow eyes.

'You had a strange dream – that's all.' He looks at me as if I am simple, a halfwit. I thought I'd mastered my temper, but I am on my feet in a moment and the razor edge of my sword is at Morcant's throat.

'Don't you ever dismiss me,' I say. Morcant doesn't blanch and the wolf doesn't blink. 'I put my life at risk by sharing this fire with you. Don't let me regret it.'

'Put the blade down, Trista,' Morcant says. His voice is as soft as carded wool, and I feel the sharp point of his short sword jabbing at my mail.

'Only when you do the same.' We stare at each other. Morcant's eyes are the steady yellow-green of the wolf's lit by a man's intelligence. I find it hard to pull myself away from them. Then, almost as if we have agreed this truce beforehand, we count to three together and withdraw our weapons as one.

'What was that about?' He is grimmer when the wolf is fully awake.

'I won't be treated like a dolt. I'm telling you the truth. I've seen you transform with my own eyes.'

'Like you saw Lucius' children?' he says and there is that hint of a sneer in his voice that boils my blood.

'Like I saw you push Lucius into the fire and bury his body under the snow.' He is about to argue but snaps his mouth shut. The wolf is sniffing the air and his hackles are raised.

'Someone is coming.'

I don't doubt him. A wolf's senses are much superior to a man's and even a woman's. I kick slush over the fire to douse it and follow him into the cover of the bushes. My spear and short sword are at the ready. I thank the gods that Morcant is a tougher man with the wolf awake. I'd rather fight beside a bestial soldier than a gentle fool.

49

CHAPTER EIGHT

Morcant's Story

The air reeks of bloodied men. They ride with the stench of corpses. The stink of smoke is in their hair, in their clothes, on their skin. Their horses are terrified and so is their dog, a war hound trained to yield to men. The female is beside me, readying her weapons with quick, practised movements. I watch her from the corner of my eye. She is straining to see what is ahead. I can't see anything but I don't need to, I can hear them. Four men – two on horseback, two on foot trailing a little way behind. I can taste them.

There's a small chance that they will pass us by – if we keep still – but it doesn't seem likely. The river draws them here– as it drew me; its rushing waters can be heard for miles.

Trista swallows hard when she sees them. I feel her whole body tense. She trembles and I don't blame her. Two against two mounted men, two foot soldiers and a war dog are not good odds. Worse, the riders are both broad, grizzled men with the tough look of veterans. I've no doubt Trista knows what she is doing but she's young and even with the mail shirt to lend her bulk, she seems slight for her height. Neither of the mounted men is wearing armour, though they have shields strapped across their backs. I note the glint of gemstones on the scabbard of the oldest man, the gleam of gold around his neck. My companion points to him and mouths 'Chief'. This is her sworn enemy? I take a closer look. He may have a torque as thick as a snake around his throat but he has no helmet, no chin guard, no mail, nothing but a singed tunic and a fur-lined cloak to protect him. The silver fur is wolfskin; my stomach churns. The wolfskin jogs a memory: I've seen this man before. He's the one who attacked Julius. It is thanks to him that I was left alone with Lucius. I've more reasons to hate him than the female knows. I glance at her. The muscles on her face bunch where she is grinding her teeth. Her sweat is soured with fear. We freeze as the war band approaches and make no sound.

It is the dog who senses us first. The female's human stink is strong. He snarls and barks and comes within ten paces of our hiding place. I'd like to finish him straight away. I want to tear his throat out with my teeth. The woman looks at me questioningly and points to the site of our campfire. If we stay where we are, we'll be cut down: we don't have room to unsheathe our swords and if we were to try we'd be more threat to each other than to our enemy. She is right. We have to take a stand. We are going to have to face them in the open. The woman leans very close to me and mouths, 'I'll frighten the horses and take the Chief.' She indicates the torque with her hands. 'You take the other one.' She mimes a stabbing action with her spear. It won't work, of course. I watch as she leans Lucius' shield against the bush. She looks at me and I realise that she intends to fight without it and means me to do the same. Fighting without a shield is at least a quick way to die. She hands me her spear then stoops to pick up a fallen tree branch, thick as my forearm, and a handful of stones.

The riders up their pace. The Chief is spurring his mount on, yelling to his men to find out what the 'blasted cur' is barking about. I don't like this man, which is good because the fierce female is about to try to kill him. She's looking at me. She's telling me to be ready. I see her breathing deeply, rapidly, building herself into the warrior frenzy of a tribesman. Her scent is no longer tainted with terror.

Her timing is good – when the men are barely five paces away she hurls herself out of our hiding place, screaming a war cry. She flings a handful of stones from her left hand right into the eyes of the nearest horse and, startled, it rears up. I follow her. Now I understand. I throw her spear to her left hand. She catches it cleanly, running towards the second horse. Bright flames bloom from the branch in her right hand and the second horse rears up. These ponies are not chariot-trained for battle and the mounted men struggle to retain their seats. My target slips gracelessly to the ground. I aim my spear carefully and take him cleanly in the chest as he falls. A surprising hit – I'm not usually that good. I don't stop to see how the woman fares – there's no time. The other two men are running towards me, their swords drawn and their mouths open as they scream war cries of their own. Screaming is a waste of breath. Real soldiers, legionaries, favour the calm deliberation of killing to order. We don't waste energy on frenzy. My own gladius, my short sword, is already in my hand, though I don't remember drawing it. It's not the best weapon for hand-to-hand combat. I feel naked without my shield, defenceless without my cohort beside me, but this is a new kind of fighting and I'm ready for it.

One of the men is shrieking at the dog to attack. I can see that the man is breathless and limping. He is already injured and hoping that the dog will do his killing for him. The dog bounds towards me, saliva dripping from his muzzle, his eyes red. I bare my teeth and growl. The sound startles me as much as it frightens the war dog. He whimpers, flattens his ears to his head, his tail between his legs, and backs away from me. That's it, little brother! Cower before your betters and trot off! The dog's response shocks the warrior, who checks his limping run. His comrade in arms is on me now too. I snarl a warning. They are wary. The dog still whimpers and keeps his distance, refusing their orders to attack me. They are no more than a pace away now. Someone cries out in agony and shock. I think it must be the Chief and one of my opponents turns away to sprint to his aid. The woman must be winning her battle.

The limping warrior's sword is raised ready to strike me, but he has no real stomach for this fight – I see it in his eyes. As he steps the final pace towards me I dance out of his way so that the first hack of his butcher's blade misses me entirely. His long shield catches me a glancing blow on the arm and that in itself is almost enough to knock me over. Now that I am closer to him I can see that his shoulder is a mess of dried blood. I can hear the agony in the timbre of his voice: the cry he gives is not of aggression but of pain. I am so close his breath is in my face. To me he already smells of defeat. I act quickly and I stab at his chest before he has time to raise his longsword a second time. I put my strength behind the thrust and time it right. He buckles. I don't flatter myself that I could better him were he fit, but he is not fit and I finish him cleanly. A mail shirt would have saved him and I am pleased that the female wears Lucius'. It might keep her alive long enough for me to help her. I grab the sword from my enemy's dead hand and sheathe my gladius. It's a while since I have held a Keltic weapon, but the length and heft and weight of it seem natural to me. It's a fine weapon with a well-honed edge and I am grateful I did not feel its deadly touch. I am alive. My blood sings with the joy of it and I run towards the woman.

She has a fighter's focus. She grunts with the effort of fending off the powerful attack of the Chief's man. It would have been easier with a shield to absorb the blows. She has nothing but her own sword to keep his blade from biting home. Desperately she parries each slashing sword stroke. She is using her own sword two-handed, bracing against the impact of each powerful hit. Thus far her blade has not shattered and she has not weakened, but she is yet to find an opening to counter-attack. She's tiring. It is in the lines of her face, the grimness in her eyes.

Her opponent wears no protective armour. I come up quickly behind him and with one clean two-handed blow hamstring him. His scream sends all the birds from the tree-tops and he crumples to the ground. She finishes him cleanly. The ground is pink where blood is diluted by slush, red and dark where it has pooled next to the fallen Chief. There are other men nearby – I can smell them. Maybe they're the Chief's reinforcements.

I yell, with what breath I have left, 'Let's get away from here!'

She nods. Her blackened mail is stained with blood,

though I don't think it is hers. She's panting with exertion. 'Thanks,' she says, letting her sword arm drop. She's lost her helmet somehow in her struggle and her face is splattered with gore. She bends over to recover her breath, gasping. Her sword is also stained and her hands tremble with weakness. She did well to fend the warrior off and without her I would have been dead within the first minute of this fight, mown down by the mounted warriors.

The Chief is not dead. He groans, a sound of such agony that I am about to kill him as I would an animal to end his suffering, but the female shakes her head.

'He doesn't deserve a swift end,' she says and I am glad that, for now at least, she's not my enemy.

CHAPTER NINE

Trista's Story

Morcant fights well enough when the wolf is roused. I stand to recover myself and watch him as he jogs towards the pony. He even moves differently when the wolf is awake. One of the two mounts has escaped but the remaining pony senses the wolf and bucks and rears in terror. Morcant looks puzzled. His frown deepens when Bric, the war dog, will not approach even though his master lies bleeding. It's true: Morcant really doesn't know what he is.

The Chief screams. I have to fight my instinct to grant him mercy. I don't think I'm cruel, but I hope he dies in agony – for Cerys and Elen and all the other slaves he brutalised. He killed my brothers too at Ragan's Field, even if his men wielded the final blows: Evan, Bryn and Kai the black-handed. He didn't kill Gwyn; that honour was mine. The Chief's cries remind me of Gwyn's torment. I find my helmet in the dirt and pull it hard down over my ears to block them out.

In my memory Gwyn will always be hale and fit and mocking me. 'Cariad, I tell you, good though you are, you'll never match a man in the killing ground.' How wrong he was.

There's no shame in shedding tears for the lost but I don't want Morcant to see me cry so I blunder after the pony, whispering the words my father used on his chariot horses. The wolf is still alert, sniffing the air and listening intently. He paws the ground impatient to be off. Morcant doesn't have to tell me that he thinks someone else is coming.

I haven't ridden for too long so my vault on to the beast's back is so clumsy I almost fall off backwards. Thankfully Morcant doesn't see this graceless manoeuvre as he is still gathering up our gear and collecting our spent spears like a good soldier. His lodged in the chest of one of our enemies, mine in the Chief's eye. The Chief howls like a beast as the spear is withdrawn and that sets the pony off again. Unfortunately his scream will carry a long way, a beacon to any of his allies still alive.

Morcant jogs after me towards the bank of the river, swollen with meltwater and white with foam. I don't try to speak over its roar but point across to the other bank. The pony bucks and rears. I have to keep stroking the warm flesh of its neck and whispering Da's magic into its ears to keep it from bolting. When we plunge into the freezing water, I am blinded by a numbing spray of icy needles. It takes my breath away. I close my eyes. I yell prayers to the goddess of the water. I have to trust to her grace and the instincts of the pony to see me across. I glimpse Morcant as he wades after me, flinching as he enters the river. Such cold could kill him.

I strain to hear sounds of pursuit but I can't hear anything but screaming above the roaring water. I think it might be in my head. Surely the Chief will be dead by now. It is my right and duty to avenge those the Chief harmed. I've done what had to be done. I say it over and over.

Morcant is blue with cold when we reach the steep bank at the river's other side. I can hear his teeth chattering as he hauls himself out. I wish I'd thought to strip the Chief of his fine, fur-lined cloak. I would have nothing of his, but there is no reason why Morcant couldn't have benefited from our victory.

Morcant glares at me and I remember to look away as he wipes himself dry and dresses himself as quickly as he can in dry clothes from his pack. I hear the distinctive bark of Bric across the river and the Chief's scream. I was wrong – he is still alive.

When Morcant is fully clothed, we head for the deep wood, where two people and a pony might lose themselves.

'Do you think there are more of them to track us?' Morcant asks. They are the first words either of us has spoken since the skirmish.

I shrug. 'I'm surprised anyone survived the massacre. He might get help from other Parisi tribes.'

Morcant is impatient.

'I can guess as well as you can. You're a seeress – can't you foresee it?'

I try to answer him but I am already tumbling into the darkness.

'Trista!' Morcant's voice is sharp. It brings me back to the moment. Thank all the gods I was only gone for an instant. The pony tosses its head and skitters out of Morcant's way as he tries to come closer to me.

'What happened? I thought you were going to fall off!'

I am slick with sweat and my heart is racing with the shock of his voice calling me back.

'I was having a vision – nothing that helps us. Something I have been seeing since childhood.' His look is questioning; even the wolf, looking at me with one paw raised as if to run, is curious. 'I keep seeing a man imprisoned. He is no one I know . . .' It's too difficult to explain. I have visions all the time and most of them make no sense. We have more urgent problems.

'You can't see if we will be followed?' I shake my head and Morcant's expression tells me clearly what he thinks of my gift. He's right.

'The Chief is still alive. If he can, he'll follow us. He'll want his revenge for what we did,' I add. Perhaps I should have finished him when I had the chance. If he survives his wounds, I know I'll never be free of him. 'I could let the pony go? That would set a false trail.'

He doesn't reject the idea so I dismount stiffly and slap the pony's skinny rump to send it on its way. It finds some grass emerging from the melting snow and begins to graze.

'Chase it away, will you?' I ask Morcant and at his approach the terrified beast runs crashing through the trees.

'That might confuse them,' I say. I am beginning to wonder if maybe the Chief's fate is bound up with my own, that there is some geas upon us. Such things can happen.

The two of us stumble on for a while before it becomes clear that we both desperately need to rest. Although I hate to show weakness, I call for a break. The look of relief on his face suggests that he is as keen to stop as I am.

I light another fire. It may well draw the attention of our enemies, but without it Morcant will be chilled beyond recovery. We squat down beside the fire together and I make another potch of grain and root.

'You know this is not the way to Armorica?'

He grins unexpectedly, showing sharp, very white teeth. 'Armorica, Brigantia – one place is much like another to an outlaw.'

'I thought you had family.'

'My mother is dead. I'm as much a Roman to her kin as I'm a Kelt to my father's. A mongrel doesn't get much of a welcome anywhere.'

I spoon the hot food into my mouth so that I don't have to reply. He's as rootless as I am.

'What about you?'

'I'm kin to the Brigante Queen – according to my father anyway. She might have need of another warrior.'

'Then you'd better get used to fighting with Rome.' I am about to ask him what he means when he asks a question of his own.

'Why were the pony and the dog so alarmed by me?'

'You know the answer to that,' I say tartly.

He has taken off his boots and is warming his feet, holding his toes so close to the blaze that he risks losing them. His feet are long and thin and I resist a curious urge to take them in my hands to warm them.

The wolf is dozing and Morcant is calmer with the wolf asleep. I notice that his strange eyes are now more grey than yellow: the gentle man is back. His voice is so soft I have to strain to hear it. He doesn't look at me. 'I almost believed you, about the wolf. Back there, when we were fighting . . . there was a moment . . . with the dog . . .'

He warms his foot and leg bindings, holding them to the

flames. 'How could it be possible? How could a man have two natures?'

It's a good question. How can a woman see the future, light fire without flint? How can bards remember a thousand tales and a Chief murder and rape without conscience? The world is full of good questions and I've no answers to any of them. I listen to the crackling of the fire, the wind rustling the treetops, Morcant's steady breath.

'I don't know how or why. I don't know what whim of which god such a thing serves.' I finish the last of my food and scrape the pot with my finger to avoid his earnest gaze. 'I've seen you change, Morcant. I swear it. And tonight you will transform again.' I shiver. I wish it weren't true but it is. I will be as much at risk from him tonight as I was last night. I'll have to be ready.

He is very close beside me. He looks stricken. It's not easy being touched by the gods. No one knows the loneliness of it better than I do. I reach out to clap his hunched human shoulder. As my fingers brush his skin, I get a jolt of strange force. I leap back away from him. The wolf starts to full wakefulness and growls at me, but Morcant's human eyes have already flashed a warning. For a moment I am assaulted by sensory information and I see what it was like for Morcant to stand before the Old One, the pack leader. The Old One growls a warning, telling him in the set of his ears, of his tail, that Morcant is not welcome. The Old One's scent sings of his virility, his power. The others are hostile and watchful, waiting to see what comes next. Then there is the she-wolf, the butt of the pack, exuding musk, signalling her interest with the set of her tail, her eager eyes.

I am stunned, unable to move or speak for a moment. It is another world, a revelation of subtle scents and sounds. For a moment I had the chance to see, but now am blind again.

'What did you see?' Morcant is aggressive. The wolf's thick pelt bristles and his eyes bore into me as if he knows that I experienced his rejection from the pack.

'Have you seen *my* children?' Morcant's smile is what anyone would call wolfish, and there is no warmth in his eyes. I shake my head.

'I've seen what you can do, Morcant. Your senses are a gift. You must be able to smell anyone pursuing us. Are there men on our trail?'

'Are you insulting me?' The look in his eye makes me reach for my blade, but then the man flares his nostrils as the wolf sniffs the air. Morcant shakes his head and looks as sheepish as a wolf can.

'There are men around, but I don't think they are tribesmen.'

That is no comfort. If they are men of Morcant's legion, fresh from murdering my fellow slaves, we may be in even worse trouble.

Morcant doesn't say anything else. He must know that ordinary men lack his sense of smell. Now is not the time to discuss it. I don't want to meet any men and neither does he. We put out the fire and collect our packs. Mine seems heavier by far than it did this morning.

CHAPTER TEN

Morcant's Story

We keep bearing north for Brigantia. I set a brisk pace. We are both exhausted but there's no point in giving in to it. We need to get away from the Parisi lands.

I'm certain that I can smell people, some distance behind us, but the Chief's men are not my only worry. I fear that I'm being stalked by a wolf. It is probably only Trista's wild talk, but I can smell the distinctive musk of a she-wolf.

'I think we are being followed,' Trista says after a while.

'Two men,' I say, 'maybe three.'

'You were not going to say anything?'

'They were a long way behind.'

We move closer instinctively and check our weapons. Wet and cold weather can play havoc with steel. As she bends down, Trista lets out a cry. I think at first that she's been hit by a spear, though I heard nothing. She falls and her pack opens and spills with a clatter of copper against iron ground.

I can't see any injury but her face is bloodless, so pale she that looks like an unpainted marble statue. I pull her helmet from her head and her red-gold hair spills around her, like dark mead. Her eyes move beneath closed lids as if she dreams. Her breath is shallow and rapid. She is as tall as I am and weighed down with her heavy mail and shield, but somehow I pull her upright and get her over my shoulder.

I half drag, half carry her to a nearby tree, as the dead are taken sometimes from the battlefield. I know that she has gone to the place of visions, that she is perhaps possessed by the spirits of the gods. I want to run. I can hear the men now and they are not far away. I don't want anything to do with the uncanny, with the dark spirits of the tribes and their thirsty, blood-craving deities, but I can't leave her. She is a dead weight and I dump her down too roughly. She doesn't even respond to my manhandling. Oh, by Mithras' balls, I can't defend us both. I unsheathe my sword anyway and plant my spear next to me. I drop my pack next to Trista and ready my shield. I strain my ears and hear fragments of conversation – in Latin. It's my own people and not the Chief. I almost laugh with relief. Then I remember. I am a deserter from their army and the penalty for that is death. When was I supposed to report? I can't remember.

Trista groans – the sound is horribly loud in the silence. She struggles to sit up. There's blood in her hair where her neck snapped back and her head hit the frozen earth. The Romans are almost upon us. I scoop up Trista's helmet and thrust it back on her head.

'Romans are coming – pretend you're ill and cannot speak.'

She nods and I wonder if she needs to pretend. She's not focusing properly and her face is now the grey-white of the melting slush.

I brush twigs and mud from my cloak and straighten up. I am not a deserter, but an incompetent scout who's lost his way. Another scouting party comes into view. They smell of fatigue and blood. I don't think I'm the only one to have run into trouble. They eye me warily. I spot the Decanus, the man in charge, right away. He's a stocky Lusitanian with the swarthy looks of his countrymen and a reputation as a brawler.

I salute him: 'Gaius Agrippa Morcant reporting, sir – scout of the Ninth. We ran into a bit of trouble with the natives and Triss here is injured – blow to the head – can't speak.' He recognises me too and something in his manner relaxes.

'Pox-faced Brit-shit tribesmen! You've heard about Caratacus and his rebels? They're all at it now. We've all had trouble lately. Can your mate walk? We're heading back to camp now.' His small group has been hunting down survivors of the hill fort massacre. The thought makes my stomach sour and I struggle to keep my expression under control. He makes some rapid introductions that I don't take in and his men help support Trista as she staggers to her feet. At least her height and lean build make her a convincing enough man.

'Bastards who attacked Julius – we sorted them out,' he says. I can smell the acrid smoke of the fire still clinging to him and I'm repulsed. Of course that's why Trista's hall was attacked! I hadn't connected the scuffle in which Julius was injured with the punitive raid on the Chief's fort. I should have done: we are on a war footing and our commander believes in letting the natives know who's boss. One Roman injury is worth a hundred or more Keltic deaths. It is one way of getting respect quickly – or so the Prefect believes.

Trista looks at me wild-eyed and suspicious. I can't translate for her, not here and now. She allows herself to be helped and I hope that they don't notice the flash of her Keltic longsword under her cloak or the flash of fury in her eyes when two men grab her arms. Does she know these are the men responsible for what happened at the fort? I hope not: I don't know what she might try to do. We have walked together, fought together and endured together but right now she is a stranger to me. I can only hope she has the wit to keep her mouth closed and her sword sheathed.

CHAPTER ELEVEN

Trista's Story

I am going to be sick. My guts quake and roil as they always do after a vision. Is Morcant taking me prisoner? He is speaking that guttural gibberish he spoke with Lucius and though I strain to listen I cannot even distinguish separate words. What is he saying about me? Should I draw my sword and end this now? I'm not sure my hand is steady enough. At best I could take the man nearest me, but I would die soon after. Anyway, I can't fight; instead I turn my head away from the armoured men and vomit into the tree roots.

The hands that grab and brace me are gentle enough and I'm not acting when I slump against one of the soldiers. This vision is hard to forget. It was full of violence, which isn't unusual, but in this vicious battle Morcant lies bleeding; blood spurts and stains his naked torso. The ghastly pallor of his face, the look in his eyes are both disturbing, but what shocks me most is my distress. He's not of my tribe – he's not even fully a man – and I don't even know if he is on my side, but I can't shake the terrible sense of loss I felt at this vision of his death.

I try to place the vision in time and space. Will it be soon? Will it be now? Here? I have spent my whole life fearing what I have seen and worrying about what have I not. I did not foresee the death of my tribe, my family, my betrothed – what else have I not seen? My betrayal by Morcant?

The men speak to me and, by their tone, not unkindly. I stare back at them in a daze. Morcant has not betrayed me. Yet.

I let the strange foreign sounds wash over me. It would be good for them to believe that I am all but finished, that I have no strength left: it is not so far from the truth. I fall into something very close to a walking doze and just manage to keep my half closed eyes, fixed on the shadow form of the wolf, wide awake and walking with Morcant.

I notice a change in all the men as we approach their camp. They stand more erect, they hoist me more upright, and the low murmur of their conversation ceases so that I can hear the noise of men labouring, sawing, shouting, bustling. I can even here a female voice high-pitched and raucous, laughing.

Fear rises like a bad taste to my mouth. I'm as sure as I can be that someone will know that Morcant did not leave their camp with a tall man called 'Triss'. What has

Morcant told them about me? I try to catch his eye, but I can see by the tension in the body of the wolf that he is too busy playing the role of the eager young soldier to risk looking my way.

We are waiting at the entrance of a well-constructed timber fort, so new that you can still smell the sawdust in the air. It is surrounded by a deep ditch and a high palisade. It is by far the biggest encampment that I've ever seen. Armed men parade on a raised platform behind the wooden walls so that they tower above those of us still on the ground. They could spear us where we stand. Scented steam shrouds a large wooden building outside the palisade. It is larger even than the Chief's roundhouse and the laughing woman is standing outside it. Her ample bosom is decorated by rows of beads and her thick hair coiled into an improbable tower of plaits upon her head. Our eyes meet and I look away. I don't know her, but she is Brigante. I am ashamed because I can guess her business here. She shouts something I choose not to hear. I don't blame anyone for doing what they have to do – the gods do not always bless us with choice – but her evident enthusiasm irks me. These men kill tribesmen.

I keep my head down and stumble as I walk. My face is beaded with sweat. I pray my escort think it is fever, not terror, that troubles me.

There are signs that some kind of walkway is being

constructed but for now the ground is muddy, rutted from the passage of many mules and carts and strewn with straw. It is very noisy. There are too many people. The air smells of cooking and the resinous scent of newly cut wood. There are other scents I don't recognise: alien spices, the taint of else-where, perfumes which transform this piece of Parisi country into an outpost of some foreign power. A market is under way. Someone has hung a brace of hares from the timber frame of a wall-less hut and there are shellfish too, past their best, and a couple of plump partridges. All the sound and bustle is hard to take in after the quiet of the last few days. I haven't seen so many unfamiliar faces since the battle of Ragan's Field. I can see that the wolf is ready to run and so am I.

The soldiers start talking excitedly again and I guess that this market is something new. A tall blonde man from one of the southern tribes is sharpening knives while beside him a woman urges my companions, in a variant of my own language, to taste the fine wine she has hauled from across the sea and the barley beer she has freshly brewed. The beer, at least, smells of home. A man is selling crude torques of base metal, bangles and brooches of copper, tinned to look like silver. He taps one of the soldiers on the shoulder and starts trying to sell him a brass wolf's-head ring. For a moment I can't breathe. My escort dismisses it, though it is a finer piece than the rest.

When the pedlar turns his attention to me, I just grunt and hope that is enough to send him on his way. I see the faded tribal tattoos snaking up his right arm and my guts churn. He is Parisi, like the Chief, and I want to draw my sword very badly – and let the gods guide my revenge. Nothing good can come from such Parisi scum. He thrusts the ring under my nose. I feel my temper surge out of my control, a wave of fury that carries me with it. I forget that I am supposed to be a sick foreigner, unable to speak our native tongue, and snarl under my breath: 'You come any closer and I'll have your arm off, you whelp of a pox-infested cur.' I see surprise in his blue eyes but he backs away.

Thank the gods my escort aren't paying me much attention but are concerned with the fort and the men guarding it. The guards' upper bodies are all encased in polished metal – as if they are not men at all. Although the sun is not strong, it glances off their armoured bodies and I'm dazzled by it. Men speak to me. I close my eyes, affecting confusion. More men come and lift me bodily. I dare not open my eyes. I stay very still until I feel myself being lowered on to some kind of raised pallet.

It is only when I hear the retreating clatter of their hobnail boots on stone that I open my eyes. I am in some dimly lit room that smells pungently of wood, sickness and spices. There is a shelf on the wall and a clay pot of oil burning in

74

offering to the image of a deity. I incline my head to it and ask for its blessing. Local gods can be fierce and it is better not to upset them. Morcant is beside me.

'Trista?'

'Where by the triple-headed god am I now?'

'You are in the valetudinarium.'

'The what?'

'It's where they treat the sick and injured.'

I want to leap from my bed at once. What will these people do when they find out that I am a tribal warrior and, worse, a woman?

'We've got to get away from here.'

Morcant nods his agreement. 'I've got to report to the Prefect later to explain about Lucius. I don't know what to tell my messmates. They already blame me because for Julius' injury. 'What will they do when they know that Lucius is dead?' He sounds lost. 'I'll be back as soon I can get away. We'll have to make a run for it.'

I don't point out that the entrance, and I presume the only exit, is guarded. There are no rotten timbers here, I am sure; everything is new. The wolf looks as despondent as I feel. His tail has dropped between his legs and his ears are flattened against his skull. He is as ineffectual here as I am.

'How have you explained me?'

'So far I've avoided it. Don't talk to anyone. I've told them

75

you hit your head and haven't spoken since. I must go – just stay still and I'll come back for you.'

Will he? One look at the wolf confirms it. Morcant cannot stay here within these walls while the wolf is awake. When he leaves, I close my eyes and then the visions come again.

CHAPTER TWELVE

Morcant's Story

I'm trapped like a shit-house rat in a pipe. I've been trained to do as I'm told and it's hard to stop now. The first thing I need to do is to delay the Capsarius, the field doctor. If he sees Trista, it'll be over for both of us. I catch him on the way to the valetudinarium. He is white-haired and dark-skinned, hunched a little against the cold. His eyes are very piercing.

'Sir,' I begin. My voice trembles. 'A legionary has collapsed in the baths. I was asked to fetch you. It's urgent, sir.'

My mouth is dry. I don't lie well. He sighs. 'I thought my day had started too easily. No – there is no need to escort me – I can find the baths in this great cosmopolitan city of ours …'. He turns round at once and I see that he already has his equipment with him. I don't believe this ruse will delay him long.

Next I need to find my contubernium, my messmates. Although I have little time, my footsteps slow as I approach the newly built timber barracks.

Marcellus, the Decanus, is outside talking to another soldier. I slip inside without him seeing me. The place smells of new wood, fish sauce, hot oil and the stale odour of men sleeping too closely together.

Julius, the injured scout, is snoring on one of the four bunk beds that line the walls. I can tell by the steady rhythm of his breathing that he is very deeply asleep. I can see even in the dimness that Marcellus' kitbag and shield are in their places against the wall and, hanging from a nail on the wall, is his pouch. He won't keep money there; his valuables are in a small arm bag, but he might keep his game pieces in the pouch and, if I am lucky, other things that would be more use to me. I tiptoe across the hard earth floor. All my senses strain. I can smell the wine on Julius' breath as he breathes out; its sourness fills the room. My fingers find the draw-string of his pouch and close over one small disc of bone. I was right; it is where he keeps the passes. With this disc I can leave the fort to enjoy the delights of the bathhouse and of the alehouse. Praise be to Mithras, and to Lugh. It is only when I have palmed two of the discs that I become aware of a third person in the room – Marcellus.

'What are you up to sneaking round in here?' He keeps his voice low and I guess that he doesn't want to provoke a scene with a drunken Julius any more than I do. I can hear the violence in his tone as clearly as if he'd shouted.

'I'm getting a pass token. I need to buy a replacement knife in the vicus and get a bath. I've been on patrol for days . . . I'm entitled.'

'There are rumours that Lucius is dead. You'd better tell me what happened, you dirty little Brit spawn. If he died because of your pissing cowardice, all you're "entitled" to is a spear through the guts and a lingering death . . .'

I slip the tokens into my pouch as he moves towards me.

'Is he dead?'

I nod, then realise he can't see me. 'Yes. He's dead,' I say.

'Bastard.' Marcellus is a big man of twenty or so, fit and lean and angry. It was a mistake to try to sneak past him. I notice that he has wound the dangling metal-decorated leather strips of his cingulum around his buckle to keep them from jangling. I take this to mean that he intends to hurt me – silently. He has something in his hand – not his sword but his pugio, his dagger – a handy enough weapon at close quarters. I know that he and Lucius were close, that they had served together in Gaul. Of all of us in this contubernium they were the only regular pairing. I fumble for my belt knife but I've lost it somewhere in the snow-covered wilds. At least I'm taller than Marcellus, with a longer reach: I'll have to make that count.

Julius snorts in his sleep and turns over. Marcellus and I both hold our breath. Will he wake? Neither of us moves until his snoring has settled again into its regular pattern. Marcellus switches his dagger to his left hand and drops into a crouch. In spite of the darkness I can see him all too clearly. He is breathing hard too so that his surprise attack is nothing of the sort. Even so I fail to dodge his punch that smacks across my jaw. He has a strong right hand, but I'm more worried by the pugio. I grapple with him. I take a couple of solid punches to the kidneys as I abandon all efforts at defence to get to the dagger. He is panting with the effort he is putting behind his blows, but I don't feel them. I use both my hands and all my force to twist his arm and wrist until he drops the dagger. It falls with a clang on the hard mud floor, but Julius doesn't wake. I could have broken Marcellus' arm. He isn't as strong as I've always supposed. He headbutts me and I go down. We are rolling on the floor now. He keeps raining punches down on me, but I protect myself as best I can until I get an opening. I fight the urge to growl. He shifts. I duck out from under him and manage to free my right hand. I hit him hard, full in the face. The blow connects with a satisfying crack. Marcellus gives a muffled cry. I'm pretty sure I've broken his nose. He staunches the blood with his cloak and drags me across the ground by the neck of my mail shirt as I scrabble to my feet. We spill out of the door together, barely keeping upright.

It is sleeting now and in moments we are both soaked and

shivering. His blood mingles with rain and runs down his face. He pulls me to him. His voice is too low for anyone else to hear.

'I know you killed Lucius, you arse-wipe, and one day we'll be somewhere without witnesses.' He straightens up and waves away the gathering onlookers. Everyone likes a fight but the officers. He's our Decanus and it would send a poor example if he was on a charge. His knuckles are raw and bleeding, but as long as no one saw him hit me, he'll get away with it. I'm out of breath too and I can't stand up. My back and side have taken some punishment, but I still have the tokens and they were worth the beating.

'Look at the state of you!' Marcellus says contemptuously in a voice pitched to be heard. He is still breathing hard and can't staunch the blood from his nose, but is hanging on to his dignity. 'Straighten up, you native bastard, you're a disgrace to the legion.' Men are staring. Everyone knows what has happened. I'd bet that the rumour mill already has me down as a cursed liability, causing the death of two of my contubernium. He glares at me and mimes slitting my throat. I don't think so. I could have had him in there, if I'd gone all out. Something in me has definitely changed.

I wait for him to march off in the direction of the bath-house and then I limp hastily to the valetudinarium. I'm still in full travel-stained kit and that raises a few curious looks. I don't know what state my face is in either, but I can taste blood and my lip feels oddly swollen and sore. There are only two centuries camped here, not more than a hundred and sixty men, and we all know each other by sight at least. Rumour of my beating at Marcellus' hand will be all round the fort within the hour. That might work in my favour. No one would be surprised if I escaped to the bathhouse to clean up and recover. All I have to do is smuggle Trista out with me.

I know as soon as I see her that she is having another of her visions. She is thrashing around like one possessed and moaning as if in the grip of the vilest of nightmares.

'Trista!' I don't dare to touch her and make the sign against the evil eye. She opens her eyes and then a moment later appears to focus on my face. I don't ask her what she's seen. By her expression it was nothing pleasant and we have trouble enough as it is.

'What happened to you?' she begins, her voice croaky.

'Shh. Don't talk. Can you stand?' She nods but doesn't move. It hurts when I bend, but I lean forward so that she can put her arms round my neck. I try not to wince as I help her to a sitting position. She has a spicy, heady perfume that fills my head with unwanted images, which remind me that she isn't a soldier and she isn't a man.

'You're going to have to walk by yourself. We can't attract

attention.' Once more she nods her agreement but seems incapable of doing anything further. She seems dazed, shocked, and when I accidentally brush her hand it is cold and clammy. I can see that under her helmet her pale face shines with sweat: she doesn't look well.

She doesn't complain, but drags herself to her feet. I collect her pack, shield and spear, which have been propped against the wall, though it's agony. She leans on me and I have to shake her free. It pains me to hold her, but I don't want to let her go.

'You have to be a Roman soldier, Trista, and a healthy one. I have a pass to get to the vicus.' She looks blank. 'I can get us out to the village outside the fort, the vicus. We need a token to be allowed out of the gates. This army is very organised. There are systems for everything.' She nods but I don't think she understands. My mother never could deal with the way my father's people had rules for everything. It's no wonder she could not stay with him.

The sleet has turned to rain by the time the two of us stagger outside. In the light of the braziers Trista looks ghastly, as if she has been battling demons in her dreams. She readjusts her helmet and her equipment.

'Will they not think it odd that we go into the vicus fully armed?'

She's right of course, but if we have the right pass no one

will question us. 'Leave the talking to me.' She raises an eyebrow and I feel a fool because, of course, we have no choice about that.

I lead the way and try to look normal; I'm not sure I know what that is any more. I can't imagine how I ever thought I belonged here among these people, these rules. It all smells so wrong. I pull myself together, nod at a couple of the men I recognise and chat loudly to Trista in the Latin that she doesn't understand.

The fort is laid out in orderly rows in exactly the same way as our temporary camps and every other fort I've ever been in. Those not on duty busy themselves with kit maintenance, dice games or sleeping. It is early yet for the evening meal, but the bread ovens are fired and already in use. I lick my lips. We still haven't eaten.

We are at the heavy, reinforced fortress gates. I know the guard slightly – he is around my age and also from Armorica. I allow myself to limp as I approach and try to smile the rueful smile of a young recruit who's just been beaten by his Decanus. Smiling hurts. I hand over the bone discs I took from Marcellus. The guardsman, Brutus, examines them carefully.

'Need a bath,' I say conversationally as he wrinkles his nose.

'Who's your friend?' he asks. Trista gives him a hard

unfriendly stare and he looks away. She can be very intimidating when she chooses. It works to our advantage.

'Oh, this is Triss from Gaul.' I point casually at her with my thumb and she gives a barely perceptible nod.

'I hear you ran into some trouble,' Brutus says. I know he's bored and ready for any conversation. I don't have time for that. It is fully dark now and the moon is so bright I can barely look at it. I can smell the night air. It is full of delicious, tempting aromas, the reek of dead things and the stench of dirty man-things. I am hungry and there are things out there I can eat. An owl hoots in the darkness and my blood stirs. When a lone wolf howls, I shiver at the sound. My muscles tremble and for a moment I feel a surge of raw animal power.

'Morcant – are you all right?'

I want to shake away this strange feeling. It is making it impossible to behave as I should. I can't answer. As I shake my head, I can almost convince myself that I feel the soft movement of luxuriant fur ruffling under my cloak. I am so hot. The man things cling to me, stinking of sheep and smoke and the acrid flavour of dirty human bodies. I have to get free of the things that tangle and trap me. I bite and tear with my teeth, rip socks and caligae, taste leather and the cold tang of oil and metal. Man stuff. I gag because the stench chokes me. There is too much of it everywhere. I stretch out my long, strong spine and the man-things no longer cling and confine. I can wriggle free of them. The sword clangs to the ground with a sharp clatter that startles me. The clean air tastes crisply of snow, of wolf and hunger. Hunger has a hard, bitter smell, bright as stripped bone.

The male cries out and the female makes a sound. I had almost forgotten her, though it is her stink that is in my nose. She makes a small mewling cry like a hare in its death throes. I remember plump flesh tearing, frail bones splintering in wolf jaws. Hot blood spurts like berry juice, sweet and wet in my maw. Hungry. Hungry. She steps back and her smell is rank with fear. Can I do that to her? She is much bigger than a hare. My mouth is wet with hunger, my wetness drips on to the ground. No I can't do that to her. I remember her. She is Trista, my ally not my prey.

I hear the lone wolf cry again and I throw back my head and howl my message: I am near, a strong, fast male in my prime, with a fine voice in my throat and a powerful hunger in my belly.

The she-wolf has come for me and I will answer her call.

CHAPTER THIRTEEN

Trista's Story

Morcant howls and he is a wolf again. There is no warning. One moment Morcant is talking to the guard and grinning in spite of his battered face, the next he changes. The man becomes the shadow and the shadow becomes flesh, fur and fierce predator's eyes. The soldier guarding the gates screams and fumbles for his weapon. My longsword is in my hand before I've thought about it. I cry out. The wolf's glance is baleful. He bares his teeth, but does not attack. Morcant the man is not asleep. I see that. It must make a difference and I trust that the wolf will not attack me. I'm right. He doesn't attack but leaps past the still startled guard, streaking through the vicus. I have to follow him.

The guard wears only a tunic beneath his body armour. He has no shield. Shock has made him slow. I thrust the pointed edge of my blade into the only weakness in his metal carapace I can see, his unprotected underarm. I feel the sword pierce then slice through his muscled flesh. I push down hard until it bites into bone and then I withdraw it cleanly. The cut is more than enough to disable him. He shrieks and falls away from me. It is too dark to see the blood flow. He can't chase me – that is all that matters – and I sprint through the gate before the rest of the fort can come to his aid.

Outside the gate there is little light and I run blindly away from the fort. Ahead I glimpse the low, lithe figure of the wolf, loping towards the distant blackness of the forest. I hear screams, the sound of stalls overturned. It is all confusion and behind me I hear the alarming, musical blast of a horn; it can only be a call to arms and I know that the soldiers are mustering. Soon I'll be pursued.

I run towards the bathhouse because it alone is lit by braziers and it's not far from the forest. It is maybe fifty paces away and already I can hear the heavy tread of soldiers behind me. Men are shouting in their ugly Roman tongue. I've a long stride and terror helps me run faster than I've ever run before. If I trip, I am done for. But I don't trip. A spear hisses past me and lands in the earth just beyond my left shoulder. I have to get out of range. I stop running straight and zigzag a little so that my position is harder to judge, but it slows me down.

Thirty paces. My pursuers are closing in on me. The

traders of the vicus, camping in their tents, watch me run but neither help nor hinder me. Perhaps they keep out of the business of the fort? In the firelight I think I see the silhouette of the Parisi tribesman. He has no reason to help me so perhaps it is an accident that his cart rolls backwards into the path of my nearest pursuers – who can say? Maybe it is the gods of this place that choose to bless me.

Twenty paces. I've got a pain in my side and my chest burns with cold fire. Morcant has gone, disappeared into the treeline. He is a beast now so why would he stay to help me? I almost stumble over my sword but right myself just in time. I can hear the men behind me cursing. It is not easy to run in all this gear. I'm almost there.

An arm grabs me, fingers sharp as claws dig into my flesh and pull me into a doorway. I don't scream: I haven't enough air. Blackness, stone walls, a small room. I panic. My sword is out and ready.

'Stop it, child.' Who would speak to me in my own language and call me child? I am ready to fight. 'Hush!' It is a woman's voice. A plump hand finds my mouth and covers it. It smells of foreign perfumes, but I obey. I bite back all my questions and my urge to stick her with my sword. I am panting, my rasping breath echoes.

'That's it. Just take your time. Here, take off your armour and put this on.' Her lips are close to my ear. She pulls me deeper inside the chamber. It is stiflingly hot. She thrusts something soft into my hand – fabric. 'They are looking for a man, cariad. Here, give me that sword.'

I hesitate. Would an enemy disarm me in this way? I don't know. 'Do you want help or not? The men are looking for a soldier. You can't escape them if you stay a soldier.'

She makes sense. I give her my sword. It is hard to let it go. I have to force my fingers to uncurl and release it. A door clicks shut and I almost cry out and then I hear her fumble with flint. I resist the urge to help. A pinprick of orange flame flickers and flares to lighten the darkness. It is the Brigante whore.

'Trista?' she says and I feel myself sway and falter as the blackness comes.

I don't think I've been out long. When I open my eyes, she is leaning over me. Her skin sags slackly. She is old. Her eyes are outlined with black lines and her eyelids shimmer blue like a dragonfly's wings. Even so there is something familiar about her.

'I didn't mean to shock you,' she says, still whispering. 'I almost didn't recognise you until I saw your reaction to this.' She pulls something from a thong round her neck and holds it in front of me. It is the wolf's-head ring. 'I thought you were dead. I thought all of you were dead.'

I still don't know who she is. And maybe the doubt shows in my face.

'Have I changed so much? Trista, it's me, Cassie, Gwyn's sister.'

I take the ring and peer at the inner surface where it is marked by a scratched design – the same mark as could be found on a hundred or so well-kept sheep in the hills of home – Gwyn's. I slip it on to my thumb. Gwyn was a big man, with hands the size of the hams we hung to smoke in the roundhouse rafters; he wore it on his forefinger. I gave it to him.

'How did you come by it?' I might be crying.

'That Parisi pedlar. I was going to buy it back from him later. When I saw you looking at it, I knew it was you even after all this time and I had to get it back for you.'

She is weeping openly now, my would-be sister. Her tears are stained black from the dark stuff round her eyes.

'He fought well, Cassie, but we were outnumbered. They took me. I didn't abandon him.' I show her my brand and try not to flinch as she presses her long-nailed finger into it.

I don't ask how she came to be here, consorting with these foreigners. I don't care to know. We embrace and I let her help me remove my soldier's clothes. She washes me with warm water from a bowl and gently dresses me. She puts a thin veil over my ravaged hair and paints my eyes as she has painted hers and still I don't ask her how she has come to this.

91

'You can't stay here for long,' she says. 'I'll be busy later but you could hide in here till morning and then we could see about getting you away.'

There is a knock on the door and I start groping around, hunting for my hidden sword.

'Stop that! Sit down there on the couch and leave me to sort this out.' She opens the door and I fight the urge to cover my entire face with my veil.

Two soldiers are at the door. They push past Cassie. They say something to her that I don't understand and she simpers. Sitting still is one of the hardest things I've ever done, but to stand would be to reveal my height.

The men speak to me. I don't like their tone of voice. One of them, with split skin above a broken nose, caresses my face with hard, callused fingers. If I had a sword, my face would be the last thing he ever touched.

'Steady, Trista, smile, love, you can be shy, but try not to look murderous,' Cassie says in my own language. I bare my teeth and hope it looks enough like a smile to pass.

The men do not linger. Cassie says something to them and they grin. She winks and gestures so that the bangles on her arms jingle and rattle and they leave laughing raucously.

'Marcellus took quite a fancy to you,' she says and I recoil.

'I can't stay around here, Cassie. I can't pretend to be . . . this.'

She sighs. 'It isn't all it seems, Trista. I'll find you something to eat and then I'll explain.'

While she is gone, I find my weapons, which she has hidden under a pile of skins under the couch – the only piece of furniture in the room. I arrange everything on my shield so that I can leave quickly if I have to. I want to strap my longsword to me but I can see that it would detract from my disguise. Where is Morcant? What will happen to him when he transforms back? I didn't think to pick up his weapons and clothes: there was no time.

Gwyn would die of shame if he could see Cassie now. He never had much patience with her; he didn't like women much, not even me.

Cassie returns with food and I try to eat decorously, but I am too hungry. Cassie has nothing and I wonder if it is her own food that I am taking, but she is as plump as a pigeon and I can feel all the bones of my ribs. She speaks softly: 'We had no one to defend us with all the warriors gone. The Parisi came and took whatever they wanted and we all ran to seek protection where we could get it. My babies did not survive that winter. I was looking to find someone who would fight the Parisi and avenge you all – instead I found Caratacus.'

It's a name I've heard before. I wipe grease from my face with the back of my hand. 'Who's he?'

'He's a tribesman from the south. He's been fighting the

invaders his whole life and he's still fighting them over in the west. I send him information when I can . . .'

'What? You're a spy?'

'Yes. You need not look so shocked. You don't have to wear a sword and look like a man to be useful, you know.' I am about to laugh until I realise that she is serious. Cassie – a spy? 'Where are you headed – once you get away from here?' she asks.

I pause between mouthfuls. 'I'm going to Brigantia, to Cartimandua's court. I thought I would offer her my sword. Da always claimed we were kin.'

She makes a noise I've never heard from her before, something between a snort and a laugh. 'If you are on the run from Rome, I wouldn't risk a visit there.'

'What do you mean?'

Cassie looks bleak. 'It's not clear that she puts loyalty to her people above her own power. She rules with the consent of Rome and that makes her eager to satisfy her foreign allies. If she found out you were on the run from Rome, I'm not sure she would admit your kinship; it is distant enough.'

I don't know whether Cassie is telling me the truth or if she merely wants to use me for her own ends.

She continues, 'Give your sword to Caratacus, Trista, and fight for all the tribes against Rome. And if you will not give him your sword at least take a message to him for me.' I'm too surprised to speak at all for a moment. I don't want to go chasing round the country for some upstart Chief I've never heard of. Why would she ask it of me?

'I am sorry for all your losses, Cassie, and I'm truly grateful for the help you've given me, but the Romans are no more my enemies than the Parisi. It wasn't Romans who killed my family and Gwyn. It wasn't Romans who enslaved me . . .' I sound more bitter than I'd intended.

Cassie hands me a red pottery beaker of sweet water and nods her understanding.

'You're young yet – you'll see,' she says. 'If they have their way, there will be no Brigante, no Parisi, only Romans and then the rest. We'll all have to obey their laws, worship their gods, pay taxes to their coffers and never be free again.'

I don't say anything.

'Say you'll take the message.'

'I'm sorry, Cassie, I . . .'

'Then I demand that you repay your blood debt. It is my right. My price is that you take my message to Caratacus.'

What is she talking about? Before I can ask she carries on.

'I know you killed Gwyn. The Parisi pedlar – he saw you. You killed my brother and I've saved you so you are doubly in my debt!'

What would she have had me do, leave Gwyn in agony? I see again the pleading look in his eyes and listen to the scream he never wanted me to hear. Even my time as a slave has not erased that memory. I'm about to argue but stop myself in time. Cassie doesn't need to know how he suffered. It does not change her rights of reparation.

'Are you sure about this, Cassie – a blood debt?'

She nods. Her face is hard under her makeup. She is nothing like the woman I remember.

'All right. You've made sure I've no choice. I'll pay the debt. Tell me what I need to remember.'

'Nothing,' she says with pride. 'I've learned to scribe – as the Romans do.' She pulls something from her breast – a fragment of bark, marked with scratches. It means nothing to me. I've been trained to remember, even though I'm no bard. I don't trust what I can't hear spoken.

'What are you talking about?'

'The Romans don't rely on the memory of messengers. They use these marks here to stand for words so that the person who gets these marks will know the words I want to say.'

'And this Caratacus can make sense of them?'

She nods.

'Can't anyone who has the knack of it read those marks?'

'Yes. That's the point.'

'Then the message could be stolen from me and given to someone else.'

'You will not let them,' she says firmly. I think she is disappointed that I'm not more impressed by her acquisition of this new, pointless skill. I take the small sliver of pale bark but, lacking her assets, I've nowhere to hide it.

'You've done well to have learned this Roman trick,' I add as warmly as I can because I would be dead without her help and I've probably not been grateful enough. Her look is cold.

'Perhaps it would be better if you left at once. The Parisi pedlar has a cart . . .'

I interrupt her. 'If he was at Ragan's Field, he's my sworn enemy!'

Her retort is fierce and exasperated. 'Have you never heard that your enemy's enemy is your friend? He's against the Romans – that's all that matters. Tribal disputes aren't important any more.'

I bite down my furious response. She was not at Ragan's Field. She did not see her family slaughtered.

'Here are some coins for your journey.' She hands me a small pouch of clinking coins then indicates my weapons and soldier's clothes lying in the middle of the floor. 'I can't keep these here.'

As if I'd let her! My cloak is not military issue but a worn plaid that ought not to mark me out as the rogue legionary. I turn it inside out to show its brighter side. I strap the sword belt tightly around my hips and I stow both the sack of coins and the strange inscribed bark within my belt pouch. She tuts; it must look ridiculous. The shield, spear, mail and other stuff is too bulky to be smuggled away easily. She frowns. 'Here, take this.' She empties the wicker basket in which she carried the food and gives me one of the skins from under the couch with which to cover my load. Even so, I realise with regret that I will have to leave my spear and shield behind.

'You will find Caratacus by the River Sabrina at Caer Caradoc out west. I know that the gods will bless you, for what you do will help save all of us.' I have no such certainty, but I kiss her painted cheek and hug her. She saved my life. I don't need my gift of prophecy to know that she plays too dangerous a game and that her life in the fort is unlikely to be a long one.

As I step out into the night, my basket over my arm and my weapons hidden under my cloak, I know that I will never see her again.

CHAPTER FOURTEEN

Trista's Story

There are armoured soldiers outside the bathhouse. It is obvious that they are still searching for me. I stoop a little to disguise my height and keep my eyes modestly lowered. Perhaps it would be a better disguise if I were bolder.

There must be fifty men or more checking the vicus. I am a woman just going about my business, an innocent bystander, curious about what is going on. I try to walk with an unhurried feminine gait.

One of the soldiers detaches himself from his cohort and wanders over to speak to me in his own language. He is carrying a burning brand to light his way. The flames dance on his armour, reminding me of the massacre of the fort. They throw the shadows of his face into stark relief, giving it a demonic look. His dark eyes glitter and I fight the urge to draw my sword. He speaks again. I can tell nothing from his tone and I have no idea what the words mean, but I gamble that it is nothing bad and force myself to raise my eyes to his. I attempt to smile. He moves closer, enclosing my waist with his arm, making it harder for me to reach for my weapon. Is that deliberate? For a moment I think he is going to accost me, then as he moves in closer I realise he intends to kiss me. He smells powerfully of fish and onions. He keeps talking, a steady stream of meaningless syllables. I ease the small dagger from his sword belt, still smiling. It is a sturdy leaf-shaped knife that glides silently in its sheath. The hilt fits perfectly in my palm, smooth as an easy promise. Luckily for him someone calls him away. He pinches my cheek with callused fingers, gabbles some nonsense and moves on. I make myself breathe. One more moment and I would have stabbed him.

I head back down the slight incline towards the glowing fires of the camped traders. The basket is heavy but I try not to let it appear so. I cover my face with my veil and slip into the darkness, away from the soldiers' torches. I am lucky that a wisp of cloud, like sheep's wool caught on a briar, covers the moon.

I find the Parisi pedlar squatting by his fire, spitting a brace of birds. He's not big, but has the lean, wiry look of a man who can take care of himself. The Roman knife is still in my clenched hand. I kneel beside him, laying my basket on the ground, and press my knife hard against the Parisi's ribs. I want to kill him. He was at Ragan's Field.

'Make a sound and I'll spit you like the Parisi pig you are,' I say. He tenses. I feel the tautening of his muscles under his tunic and I know that this one will fight back. I'll have to impose my will on him quickly before he has time to think. 'I need your mule and your cart. In return I might let you keep your worthless guts inside your skin.'

He gets slowly to his feet. With my left hand I remove his sword belt. It clatters to the ground – a mistake. The sound is loud. I expect to hear soldiers surround me, calling out their threats, rushing at me so that I am surrounded. I count ten heartbeats. Nothing happens. The pedlar is likely to have other weapons hidden about his person but I don't have time to search him. I need to keep him moving, keep him unsettled. I prod him again and keep my voice hard. 'Keep your hands where I can see them. We are going to walk towards the cart and you will give no sign that anything is amiss or I will kill you before you can summon help.'

I haven't thought this through. He will have to harness his mule and that is such a strange thing to do at this time of night he's going to attract attention. Why would a pedlar leave the vicus at dead of night with a woman?

'I hope you know what you're doing with that dagger, cariad.' The pedlar's voice is confident, his accent so like that of the Chief's that I find myself growing angry at its sound. I know that he has been taken in by my dress, that he thinks he can take me; he is waiting for his chance.

I press the knife viciously against his back. Fear and anger are making me jumpy and overeager: a small amount of blood seeps through his tunic. I pick up my basket. He doesn't say anything else but guides me to the cart past other firesides, other traders. Clever.

They greet him, or I think they do, as none of them says a word I understand. I move my knife to his side and sidle up close to him, so that our hips touch. I lean against him so that my mouth is pressed against his ear.

'Put your arm round me,' I hiss, 'like we're lovers.' His grip on my shoulders is firm. I giggle loudly, or at least that's what I try to do. I was never one for giggling so the effect is not quite what I intended. Anyway, it works, people laugh and whistle, and I try for that giggle again. We weave through the encampment a little drunkenly but I keep the knife steady. I see the Roman soldier who accosted me earlier. I duck down and I bury my head in the Parisi's neck and stagger even more obviously. The Roman does not approach.

We reach the cart. The Parisi may have a weapon hidden there. I have to give him space to hitch the mule; it is his best chance of grabbing a knife and turning on me. The clouds clear from the face of the moon and the night becomes brighter. I unsheathe my longsword. His eyes widen when he sees me. Any tribesman can recognise a warrior from the way they hold a sword. I'm a warrior and now he knows it. He doesn't make me prove it. I force him to sit beside me on the narrow seat. 'Head west,' I say. 'You're coming with me.'

CHAPTER FIFTEEN

Morcant's Story

She waits for me in the hidden places of the forest. How could I have forgotten her?

It is good to leave behind the confusion of the man stink, to leave behind the noise that fills my ears but tells me nothing I need to know. I run from the fires that distort the night and stench of smoke to the cool of the dark and a world of scents and senses. I run to her. She has tracked me all day, leaving behind the Old One, becoming a lone wolf for me. The scents of her journey cling to her fur. I drink in the history of her long day. It is in my nose and on my tongue: the battle and the spilled blood, the river and the great cold, the forest, the man-place of cut trees. She has watched and waited. When I thought I was alone, she was always there. I let her guide me, teach me how to listen to the scurrying of small creatures, to track their distinctive smell, follow her lead and make the kill. Blood. Meat. My mouth is full of the taste, my belly is full of the goodness, my nose is full of the she-wolf. She delights in my success as if I were her cub. I'm not her cub. I know what she wants of me and am happy to give it. She is mine to hunt for and to defend, as I am hers.

Then here, where we feast, I catch the pungent female odour of the two-legged female and I remember: I am not whole as the she-wolf but a broken unnatural thing. It hurts to know this, but I can't ignore it. It is like a thorn in the soft pad of my foot. I am a two-legged creature as well as a four-legged one and my pack is both the she-wolf and the two-legged female. I owe loyalty to the hunter and to the fire-maker. I can taste the two-leg's smoky, spicy scent in the wind. I should run after her. My she-wolf does not want this. She nips me and growls, but follows anyway, as I knew she would. It is up to me to keep my pack together. I know that finding the two-legged female is important and worth the anger of the she-wolf. She needs me.

She is not hard to find. She travels noisily. She is with a male whose scent I remember from earlier in the day. He smells of the smoke of campfires, of the loamy earth of many places, of the taint of metal, of blood and of ash.

We are not far away when my two-leg, the fire-maker, Trista, screams. The fur on my neck rises and I run as if I flee from fire. My she-wolf is not more than a pace behind. We are fleet of foot and fierce in fighting. The male will not do her harm. He has the sharp tooth that will bite her. No. He has a dagger that might cut her. She is already fighting him, struggling to get at her sword. Kicking out and screaming at him.

'Cassie's wrong. You're not on her side. You're the midden-born pox-ridden Parisi scum I knew you were!' Her scent is overlaid with fury. She might beat him on her own, but it isn't certain.

I growl. I want to tear out his throat and gnaw at his innards. I could snap his neck with my jaws, shred him with my teeth. I want to taste his warm blood. I will not let him get to Trista. He turns to me and I smell his fear. He runs. I start after him but the she-wolf is cautious. We've eaten well and she has no interest in a chase without a kill. She doesn't kill what she can't eat. She doesn't think men are ever worth the chase. I can see that in the way she hangs her tail and tilts her ears. We will let him go. For now.

'Morcant!' Trista smells of crude perfumes, of oil and the hot tang of the bathhouse. She does not smell of blood. She's not hurt. I taste the skin of her arm with my tongue. She is salty and sweet at once.

'I'd like to weave a basket with his guts,' Trista says. She is rubbing her wrist, where he must have twisted it to wrench her weapon from her hands. I know that she is irritated that he bested her. 'I didn't think you'd come back. Thank you.'

Her voice trembles and water comes from her eyes. I remember that this means she is distressed. She is not the only one: my she-wolf retreats.

I am torn between the two of them because they both want me. I hesitate. Trista surprises me by burying her face in the fur of my back. I feel the whole weight of her pressing down on me. She does not usually behave this way. It is as if she is sick or injured and I can't leave her.

'It's all gone wrong, Morcant. I don't know what I'm doing.' It's hard to hear what she is saying as she is mumbling into my back.

I can't do anything to help her. I have no arms to hold her so I twist my head and manage to lick the bare flesh on her neck to let her know that I am here and listening. It is odd that her skin is so smooth and bald; it tastes of perfume there, sickly and sweet. I do not react.

The man who got away will bring more men. I know this and she must know it too. She needs to keep moving so that they can't catch her. I make a noise that the wolves know means 'Danger, keep running.' She pats my neck as if it were a cry for attention. I nudge her but she sinks to the ground.

'I can't go on. I need to sleep.' She would never make these pitiful sounds of weakness if I looked like a man and the more I am with her the more like a man I feel. My she-wolf has loped away in disgust. Can her keen nose detect from my scent that I am becoming more like the two-legged hunters she despises?

The mule thrashes around in his harness. There is some good eating on him. His frightened noises rouse Trista from her hopeless state. She stands up again and wipes her face on her shawl so that all the paint she is wearing smears across her face. It changes her look but not her smell. She mutters soothingly to the mule and I find myself oddly relaxed by the gentle calm of her tone. Perhaps this too is her gift. She sees what is not there, she lights fires and she gentles restless beasts. She releases the mule from the hard burden of the cart. I don't like this cart. It is cluttered with the objects of the pedlar's trade. I can smell old blood on the clothing and the lingering trace of fear that has worked its way into the very weave of the cloth. I wonder where the pedlar acquired these wares. He has spent time in places best avoided. His things leave a bad taste in my mouth.

Trista pulls the cart off the track and under a tree. Her strength surprises me. She is not weak. She tips the cart to make a barrier against the wind and makes a camp for herself a little off the track. She takes little time to gather damp sticks. No sooner than she lays them on the ground, she kindles a flame. I am not afraid of this fire because it is hers. She made it and she can control it. Though the scent of the burning wood makes my eyes water and fills my nose with the heat and a pungent odour of scorching, I am drawn to lie by her side.

She runs her hands through my fur, and I don't even snarl. She is Trista and she can do whatever she likes.

CHAPTER SIXTEEN

Trista's Story

I touch the thick fur around Morcant's neck and, when he does not snarl, I grow bolder and stroke the luxurious coat on his back and flanks. I can feel the pump of his heart beating through his skin as if he has been running. I want to bury my head in his pelt but I resist. His fur smells of the hounds of home, of my father's hearth and of childhood. His breath smells of blood and I don't mind. I've grown used to that smell.

'Morcant.' I surprise myself by whispering his name again. The fire's orange embers flare into yellow flame and I feel his powerful muscles tense under my hands, ready for flight. His eyes are silver mirrors of light. I do not mean to say it but I do. 'Don't go.'

He nuzzles his heavy head against my chest as if he truly were one of my father's dogs, almost knocking me over. Cautiously, I brush the fine, soft hair above his eyes with my fingers and he closes his eyes. Encouraged, I scratch the tufted fur behind his ears. He settles down beside me. I groom him as well as I can, using my nails and freeing the small twigs and dried pine needles that have caught there. I pat his strong back and he acknowledges me with a flick of his tail. I sleep, breathing in the stale scent of his breath, matching my own breath to his rhythm, and I sleep well.

It is some time after dawn when I finally awake to find myself staring into the clear grey eyes of Morcant the man. His hair is plastered damply to his head. He is filthy and naked and the skin of his neck and bare shoulders is tinged with blue. He is shivering. Has he been waiting for me to wake up?

Grudgingly, I unwrap my cloak from my own shoulders and throw it at him. It is raining again, a relentless chill drizzle that soaks through even the thickest wool.

'You were right,' he says through chattering teeth, 'it's just like you said. I'm a shape-changer.' I nod and bank up the fire to warm him. Without the cloak I am shivering too. Cassie's garments were not designed for warmth.

Morcant looks at my coloured silks and scowls. 'Why are you wearing that thing?'

'I met someone I once knew. She helped me escape.'

I don't want to explain. Now in the dawn light I can't believe I let her force me into this stupid mission. I don't care about Caratacus. Every time I close my eyes, I see things that are not there. Morcant bleeding, fire blazing, the Parisi pedlar burning from the inside. I move as if I'm balanced at the edge of a precipice, as if at any moment I could fall into a pit of endless visions. I feel as if my very soul is shaking.

I stretch out my hands in front of me – they tremble like an old woman's. It is perhaps as well I have no spear for I'm not confident that I could throw it straight.

There are some things in the bottom of the cart – a sack of spare clothes, an end of cheese, as well as the Parisi's wares.

I hand the sack of clothes to Morcant who wrinkles his nose. 'It smells of the Parisi.'

'It's that or freeze,' I say. I want my cloak back. He makes the sensible choice and dresses while I rummage through the pedlar's assortment of metal goods. They are so poorly made that almost all of them have rough, unfinished edges – anyone wearing one of his torques would have nicked the skin of their neck in no time. It is a wonder that he did any business. I can't find anything else that belonged to my people, the family and friends slaughtered in battle at Ragan's Field. He was there all right. He told me that much when I had a knife in his guts, but there is nothing in all these trinkets worth keeping.

Morcant looks different in the Parisi's spare clothes. There's one thing for sure: no one would believe him to be a

Roman any more. I half expect to see tribal tattoos snaking up his arms, but his arms are bare, almost hairless, with only the small wolf mark to show his loyalties. He sees me looking at it and laughs. 'It couldn't fit me better, could it?'

He rubs his stubbled chin with a grubby finger. 'I'm sorry I didn't believe you – before. I don't know, but this . . . thing only happened to me when I was a child and I thought it was a dream. It's never happened like this.'

Perhaps that's true. I know he thinks I have something to do with his change. I can see the thought written plainly on his face, but he doesn't say anything. The wolf is sleeping and this is Morcant's gentle time. He helps me right the cart.

'Trista. I can't be like this.'

'What do you mean?' I say carefully.

'I can't be the beast. I can't feel what he feels, live the wolf's life. It's all wrong . . .' His voice is so quiet I have to lean towards him just to hear. He looks haunted, desperate.

I put my hand out as if to touch him and then pull it back.

'But the things you can know as a wolf – the smells, the sounds. Isn't that worth it all?' I can't forget the moment I touched Morcant and experienced the world through the nose and ears of the wolf. I don't have the words to describe the sensations. Such insights would give a warrior such an advantage.

Morcant doesn't feel the same way. He shakes his head.

'You don't know what it's like! I've got no control. One moment I'm me, the next I am lost. I find myself in places and I can't remember getting there or worse, I'm the beast and I think and feel and . . .' he pauses, lowering his voice so that I strain to hear him, 'and I act like a beast . . .'

This time it is he who reaches out to touch my hand. I know exactly what it's like to have no control, to be lost. I've lived my whole life that way. Would I give up my seeress's gifts if I could?

'Morcant, you're new to it. You get used to it.'

'No, no.' He shakes his head fiercely. 'The druids know about such things, don't they? They can cure me of this affliction, can't they?'

'I don't know. Your ability is a gift of the gods. Even the druids do not set themselves against their will.'

'Help me, Trista. Take me to the druids.'

He squeezes my hand and looks at me earnestly: something hard in me softens. No one has looked at me like this before.

'You could go to the Sacred Isle, to Mona, but the druids there may choose not to help you.' Who knows what druids will do? They are as hard to predict as the weather and as powerful.

Morcant is smiling at me as if I've promised to cure him myself, and I haven't. I can't go to Mona.

'You'll come with me?'

There is a look of almost puppyish enthusiasm on his face. I adjust my sword belt.

'I can't go to Mona.'

'Why not? Maybe the druids could help you too?'

'No, Morcant, they won't. If you go, you'll go alone.' I don't want to tell him about the blood debt or my promise. I don't want to tell him that my father ran from Mona and still had nightmares about it years later. It is the centre of our religion and the only place I know where people might understand his plight. He lets go of my hand.

'Where will you go?'

I don't want to answer. I shrug and wipe my face. My hand comes away stained with colour. I had forgotten the paint that Cassie made me wear. I dampen the corner of my cloak in a puddle of rainwater and scrub away at my face with it.

'You've missed a bit.' Morcant uses his fingers to wipe the pigment from my face. 'It makes your eyes look huge,' he says, and I don't know if that is a good thing or not.

I find it hard to pull my gaze away from his. He has an injured look, like a whipped hound, and I feel myself beginning to flush. He turns his attention to his fingers. I've never noticed how strange fingers are! They are so dextrous, so flexible, so sensitive. He touches my cheek with the tip of his

115

forefinger. He brushes my skin so lightly I shiver. I don't dislike the feeling.

'I'd hoped you'd stay with me – the beauty and the beast!' He laughs a little wildly as if some part of the beast remains with him even when the wolf is asleep. He doesn't need to make fun of me.

'We should go,' I say. 'We need food. Maybe there's a village somewhere near? Unless you can hunt?'

He looks aghast at the suggestion. Perhaps it is because I was raised as a warrior and grew up with hounds that I admire what a wolf can do.

I kick mud over the fire and cover our tracks with a tree branch. I put on my mail and helmet to save the bother of carrying it. I know it looks ridiculous with my draped tunic and thin-soled lady's sandals but the kit is easier to wear than it is to carry. Morcant looks at it enviously.

I leave the cart and the pedlar's ill-made trinkets but I take the mule, holding his halter. He keeps well away from Morcant. As we walk, I tell Morcant an edited version of my rescue by Cassie, but I'm on edge. If I were a Roman, I wouldn't let us escape.

'What's wrong?'

'I think we're being followed. It's a pity the wolf is asleep – we could use his sharp senses.' Given the way he feels about the wolf, I probably shouldn't have said that. He tenses.

'I don't need the wolf!'

'Shhh!' I hiss at him. I can hear something – a snapped branch a way back, behind us. I'm sure of it. There it is again: the sound of someone moving. I glance back at Morcant to find him glaring angrily at me. His eyes are tinged with yellow. The wolf is back.

Morcant stops walking to listen. His shadow wolf cocks his ears, tilting his head, testing the air. Morcant the man does much the same. I am right. There is something there. I feel a familiar weakness and I pray to the god that cursed me with the gift of prophecy – keep my vision clear for a time at least.

The tree coverage is not dense here. The ground is uneven but essentially flat.

Morcant's face looks grim. 'They're Roman. Any bright ideas?' he murmurs. With the wolf awake his tone is sharper.

We are poorly armed and he hasn't even a spear. 'We fight?' I say.

'There are eight, maybe ten, men?'

'Then we die.'

'And what's the point of that?'

'Warriors fight. It's what we do.'

His yellow eyes are quizzical. 'Wolves don't fight battles they can't win. They submit and bide their time.'

'I'll not surrender.'

'Then we hide.' He does not expect me to argue and I don't, but I can't say I like the idea. My blood is already pumping, ready for the fight. Morcant guides me into the thickest undergrowth which is still sparse. He ducks down into a half crouch, moving with an easy, loping grace. I feel awkward. I'm not good at stealth. I take off my helmet, pull my cloak over my mail and Morcant signals for me to cover my hair. He pulls me down on to the damp ground and I lie flattened in the grass. There are still patches of snow lingering. I don't see how we can be missed.

I strain to hear the sound of approaching footsteps. They are closer and I can hear the chink of metal against metal, the low whisper of voices. We wait.

CHAPTER SEVENTEEN

Morcant's Story

The men are no more that a couple of long strides away. I can see their clean-shaven cheeks, scent the residual oil from the baths on their skin, the old-wine stink of their breath and the rotten smell of their long-ago breakfasts. They are a scouting party, probably sent to track and pursue us, but I can tell by the way they are moving that they think their task pointless – another stupid army drill. We did a lot of them in the Ninth. Their talk is of women and home. They are not paying too much attention to their surroundings.

I think we'll get away with it. I think they'll pass us by. Then Trista's stupid mule wanders into view – still wearing his halter. Mules do not stray into forests on their own and the men are instantly alert. It is not one of the many army animals; it does not bear the brand of the wolf. I watch the Decanus check carefully. It's the Parisi pedlar's beast and not only are the bridle and halter of native design, but they are bright with ribbons and jangle with all the Keltic charms attached to the harness for good luck. Mithras' balls! Why didn't we tie up the mule? The Decanus issues a terse command, but it's barely necessary. The men shut up, straighten up and become soldiers. I can see them scanning the land with practised eyes, instantly ready for action. They remove their shields and arrange themselves into a better defensive formation. Stupid, pissing mule.

The men unsheathe their swords and start to fan out warily to look for the mule's owners. Our hiding place will not bear careful scrutiny. They'll find us and Trista will fight and then she'll die because, in spite of her time as a slave, she doesn't know how to submit. The stink of Rome is so strong I almost sneeze. I start to crawl backwards away from the men. I hear Trista gasp and whisper something, yanking at my cloak, but I'm not listening and the cloak comes away in her hand. She stifles a cry as I lose all that encumbers me. I try to do it silently. The sweaty wool of my tunic flops to the ground with barely a sound. I step out of it, keeping my body low. I slink forwards so that my belly almost scrapes the ground. I have to leave Trista behind.

I can smell deer nearby and I know that the thought of fresh venison will distract these men as nothing else could. Unfortunately it distracts me too. I picture myself biting into the succulent flesh of a doe and I find myself salivating. I have to think of something else, of my need to redirect these men so that Trista might get away. I haven't much time. The men are shouting to each other, frightening away all the wild animals and the other, dark things of the forest that I try not to see. The Romans know exactly what they are doing. One of the men is walking in Trista's direction. His eyes are fixed on the ground, his sword is out. I break cover and run.

Someone cries out, but my ears are back and I'm running so fast I know they won't catch me.

All the men's shouting has woken my mate. Her musk calls to me and I let her know that I'm here and needing her. She is still angry with me – I can see it in her stance – but she does what I ask and we two herd the deer back towards the Romans. The deer are skittish and reluctant to head where we want them to go, but they fear us more than they fear the men. One of them is lame and we might be able to take it down. I know the she-wolf is thinking the same thing. I have to concentrate on Trista, her special scent, her fighting spirit, her need for me, so that the painful emptiness in my belly does not distract me.

The she-wolf is fleet-footed. I have to work hard to match her. She has already isolated the weak doe, but the deer is too big for her to take down on her own. She needs me too and even the prospect of meat will not tempt her to go within sight and spear range of the men: she was hit once by a glancing spear-blow and will not risk it again.

I hesitate. I think we could take the doe, but these beasts can run and the chase might take us miles from this place. I have to go back to the place I left the female, I mean Trista, to be sure she is safe. I make a sound that is between a howl and a bark to tell the she-wolf that I'll be back. I run beside the herd, still driving them with my powerful scent, but keeping my distance so that the Romans will see them before they spot me. I find what shadows I can and stay in them, trusting to the subtle shadings of my own pelt to keep me hidden in this place of winter greys and browns.

The herd is not large, but their hoofs are loud in the forest and I know that there is not a man in the army who doesn't love a haunch of venison.

I see Trista at once, still cowering in the undergrowth. The shawl that should cover her head has fallen down so that her bright hair shines like a fiery beacon if you know where to look. One of the soldiers is so close that I think he must have spotted her. I drop to the ground watching. If he gets within a spear's length, I will pounce.

The deer are confused with a wolf behind them, a wolf alongside them and men in front of them, and they run the only way they can. The Decanus yells and all the men focus on trying to spear a dear. They stand little chance but that does not stop them. The young male nearest to Trista sheathes his sword and runs for the herd, putting down his shield and picking up his spear as he goes. I hope Trista has the wit to stay still. The men are still alert and she, unlike the running deer, is easy to spear. She hazards a small move-ment – lifting her head just high enough to see what is happening – and then drops back down.

The Decanus has the mule and the group move on. I wait until I judge they can no longer hear us and then double back to see how the she-wolf fares with the injured doe. Trista can take care of herself.

We run, the she-wolf and I, we exhaust the deer and then together we bring her down, sharing the kill. She gives me the choicest parts of the innards, the soft and juiciest morsels and then we eat all that we can until we can barely move. When we are both satiated, I take a large hunk of meat to carry in my mouth to give to Trista. The she-wolf slips away, her fury evident in every line of her body.

She seems small when I finally catch up with her. If I were to stand on my hind legs, I would tower over her, which is strange because when I am a man we are the same size.

She approaches cautiously. She looks exhausted, out of breath, but otherwise unharmed. She bends over to catch her breath, resting her hands on her knees and I realise she has been running at full pelt. Four legs are faster than two, they can outrun a deer and tear out its heart.

I place the raw meat at her feet and then hurry back to my mate.

CHAPTER EIGHTEEN

Trista's Story

The wolf is huge, bigger than ever, a great grey and tawny beast, his muzzle stained with blood, his breath stinking of offal. At the same time, I want to run from him in terror and throw my arms round his neck in gratitude. He saved me. I would have died in the woods if he had not turned wolf and created a diversion. It was a man's plan to make such good use of the wolf's body. Morcant the man, the pale shadow of the vital flesh-and-blood wolf, is awake and partly in control. It is hard to see him in the afternoon light, but his smile warms me. I'm sure that he didn't know he could transform in the daytime and neither did I. In all the stories I can remember of a druid shapeshifting, none took place in the sunlight.

I watch the wolf lope away into the distance until I am alone. This sudden daytime metamorphosis is yet another important thing I haven't foreseen. I have the most useless of gifts.

I take the bloody meat and wrap it in Morcant's tunic. I'm not yet so hungry that I can eat raw meat and I dare not build a fire here where the Romans could return. I am hungry, of course I am, but more than anything I'm glad to be alive. Birds sing and shafts of bright sunlight pierce through the treetops dappling the ground with alternating light and shadow. The air is sweet with the scent of rotting leaves and the damp loamy smell of the earth. The gods of the forest are gracious and I whisper my thanks.

By dusk I'm less grateful. My feet are blistered and I'm hungry enough to slice strips of raw venison with my sword to chew as I walk. I'm grateful for a strong set of teeth. I take stock. I have very little idea of where I am. I cannot walk to the River Sabrina, or at least not easily. We might be in Brigante lands by now, but I cannot be sure. Our lands are extensive and change hands with regularity. It doesn't matter. The time has come to beg, buy or bully my way into getting help. There is a limit to how much I can achieve alone and I've reached it. I need a guide or at least some advice and directions on the best way of finding Caratacus. I need a horse, some warm and suitable clothes to wear and most of all I need to rest. I am hanging on to the here and now by the thinnest skein of the finest yarn ever spun. I dare not stop battling for a moment or the visions will overwhelm me. Morcant, I need you. I want to call out to him, but I know that would be stupid.

The forest becomes another world after dark, a place of hidden things, of mysteries and dense textured shadows. I keep seeing things out of the corner of my eye, monsters and ghouls from the druids' fireside tales. Perhaps I am over-wrought with the effort of not having visions, but now that I've known companionship I don't want to spend a night here alone. I hear a sound, a movement behind me. The hairs on the back of my neck lift and I draw my sword. I strain my eyes in the growing gloom. It occurs to me that in carrying a lump of raw meat around I'm tempting every carnivore in the area. 'Who's there?' My voice shakes and it is probably stupid to make a noise, but I am not thinking rationally.

'Trista!'

It is Morcant returned to himself again and hiding behind a tree. I feel a surge of joy and relief. I sheathe my sword and walk towards him holding out my cloak. Our fingers touch briefly as he takes it from me, but there is no terrible vision, just the steady warmth of his hand. I am loath to take mine away.

He wraps himself in the cloak and emerges from his hiding place. He should look ridiculous: the cloak reaches only to his knees and reveals too much muscular, hairy leg. There is mud in his hair and a long scratch down his face. He doesn't look ridiculous; he looks magnificent and he is smiling. There are lots of things I want to say but all I manage is: 'What happened to your face?'

'Another wolf.'

I don't have to ask more. I see that he won that fight; it is in the set of his shoulders, in the shadow wolf's high tail. He exudes a new confidence, even happiness. For some reason I'm irritated by that. I'm hungry and tired and far from happy. Only I'm smiling too. He speaks and even his human voice now has the deep growling resonance of the wolf.

'I've had a look around. That Roman troop has moved on and is heading away from us. I think we're safe for the moment.'

'Good. That's good.'

'There is a village a way over there.' He points north. That's useful information too. There are benefits to travelling with a wolf. There are more benefits to travelling with Morcant.

'Thanks for . . . you know, distracting them.'

He shrugs as if it were nothing. 'Did you know you were turning?'

He shakes his head. He still holds his hand as if it were a paw. This Morcant does not waste words.

'I needed to run and I run better as a wolf.' All trace of his guilt and distress has disappeared. This Morcant seems proud of the wolf. Perhaps he only hates being the beast when the wolf is asleep?

'We have to go into the village. I need better clothes, supplies.'

'I can hunt. We should stay away from people, they only

bring trouble. The village could be Parisi. What if they are allies of the Chief? What if they're allies of Rome?'

'It's risky, but I don't know where we are and I need help to get where I need to go.' He doesn't ask me where that is. I've yet to tell him how my plans have changed.

'I don't know how or when I'm going to turn, Trista,' he says. 'This time it happened because I needed it to. Other times . . .' He shrugs, making even that gesture look wolfish. 'I can't promise that I won't turn wolf in the village. When the wolf is with me, we are one – as a beast or as a man – it feels the same.' He looks at me with wolf's eyes. Slowly and deliberately, he takes my hand.

'You are one,' I say and cover his grubby, awkward human hand with mine. I press down on his long fingers so that they curl over my own, as a man's hand can and a wolf's paw can't. 'Without the wolf you are not fully yourself. He is part of you. You are one soul, two natures.'

'Is that true?'

'It's what I learned from the druid.'

'Pity you learned nothing more useful.' He squeezes my hand very gently to take the sting from his words. I am very aware of his human body so close to me, and of his animal body somewhere nearby. He came back for me. Twice. Nothing else matters.

It is too far to travel to the village so we make camp. I

build a fire and cook the venison. I've never tasted anything more delicious. It's so long since I've eaten meat – there was none in the Chief's hall. I'd almost forgotten how good it tastes. With every mouthful I feel myself growing stronger. Morcant eats nothing. The wolf has had his fill.

The wolf falls asleep first. I gather he had good hunting. I can see his silvery outline in the firelight lying prone and breathing deeply.

Morcant's face softens as the wolf sleeps. The change is subtle but I'm beginning to know him now and I notice at once. His voice is lighter without the base notes of the beast. He sounds younger and speaks more tentatively.

'Did you mean what you said? Am I really only a half man without the wolf?'

'I didn't say that.'

'I think you did.' He sounds hurt.

I put more wood on the fire. We are sitting close together for warmth and share the one cloak we have between us. He has grown silent, brooding. I'm too tired to speculate on the nature of a werewolf. I'm so tired I'm struggling to keep my eyes open. 'Morcant, how many werewolves do you think I know?' I sound impatient. I don't mean to.

'One?'

'Exactly. I know you. I watch you and draw my own conclusions. I may be wrong.'

'You said it's what the druid said.'

'Our druid was old and spoke as much nonsense as sense. I can't talk about this now. Who will take first watch?'

He volunteers and gives me the cloak, insisting he will be warm enough by the fire. I curl up next to him as close to the blaze as I dare and let myself fall into a deep pit of sleep.

He lets me sleep for most of the night. I wake just before dawn, stiff and cold, like some garment left out to dry on a frosty day. I'm surprised my limbs don't crack as I move. His face is grey with fatigue.

'You should have woken me.'

'You were exhausted, and I wanted to think.'

I'm not sure I want to know what he thought about. I'm not going to Mona whatever he says. I insist he naps for a time and for all his protestations he falls instantly asleep. His face in repose is beautiful. It starts me thinking about Gwyn and then I have a vision of the unknown man again, but it doesn't last long and is not violent: the man is flogged but doesn't die. I come back to the present moment suddenly in a muck sweat and have to leave the fireside to be sick in the bushes. I am not reliable on watch duty, whatever I pretend. Luckily we are not attacked and I know I won't tell Morcant of my failure, but the wolf is awake and watching me. He knows.

The sun is already high before we set off and, with the

wolf's return, Morcant's dark mood lifts. He doesn't make a fuss about guiding me towards the village, in spite of his reservations. In fact he is eager to be off and doesn't so much walk as bound across the rough terrain. I get the sense that he wants to run and is held back by my stiff-legged plodding.

We haven't been walking long when we come across a stream where I can fill my canteen and wash. I tidy my hair with my hands and remove my mail. Underneath that metal shirt my flimsy, yellow-coloured Roman stola is black with oil. However I arrange it, the fabric is filthy and I know I look neither respectable nor Keltic. My hair is shorter than a tribesman's. I cover it with the grubby red-trimmed veil, now slightly damp and creased. I do not remove my sword and sword belt.

'How do I look?' I'm not fishing for a compliment. I just want to know if I look too strange in my odd Roman gear to be acceptable to my own kind.

'Like a goddess,' Morcant says earnestly and I almost believe him. I can feel myself flushing, then he adds, 'But the stola is a bit dirty and looks very strange with the sword.'

'You're not having it,' I say. Of course. He wants to carry the sword.

'It would make for a better disguise. Roman women do not wear swords.'

'I'm not trying to be a Roman woman but a tribeswoman

and we do wear swords. I know you need a sword, but you're not having mine.' I know I sound crosser than I intend but I am annoyed with myself. Warriors do not blush.

He wants to argue, I can tell. I bundle my mail shirt and helmet together, cram them into my pack and make him carry it.

'Look, you're the one who lost his sword, not me. I am the tribal warrior, not you. I'm keeping my sword.'

I can see that he accepts that argument but he doesn't give up easily.

'It will look strange – a woman with a sword, a man without.'

'People will assume you are my slave. It will be safer that way.' I rearrange my hair under the shawl to give a womanly impression. I'm not sure I succeed.

The village is further than he thought – two legs are slower than four as he reluctantly admits when we still haven't reached the village by midday. The rain which began to fall soon after dawn has turned us both into silent, miserable creatures.

He smells the village some time before we arrive. He pulls a face.

'What is it?'

'People living close together reek, you know.'

'What – and wolves don't?'

He shrugs. I nag. 'Don't sniff or anything when we get there and don't march like a soldier – try and look a bit beaten. We want their help.'

He looks far from beaten, in spite of the wildness of his hair, the dark smudge of his growing beard. His eyes are bright with the animal light of the wolf and the intelligence of the man. He walks with the kind of graceful swagger I haven't seen in him before. He doesn't seem like a slave. I want to suggest that he sends the wolf away, but I can't. This is the man I would want at my side should there be trouble. This is the man I want at my side even if there is no trouble.

CHAPTER NINETEEN

Trista's Story

The village – no more than five large roundhouses – is protected by a palisade and two young boys act as sentries. I can't tell whether they are Brigante or Parisi. When they see us coming, they raise the alarm and by the time we reach the gate there is a small reception party of young men with spears, led by a huge tattooed warrior with a long, greying moustache. It takes an effort to keep my hand from my sword hilt. I can't fight all of them. We are coming to trade, not to fight. I take a closer look at the big man. He is muddy from labouring at some task in the rain, but the torques that he wears around his neck and on his arms are gold and of fine workmanship: he is no farmer. Thank Lugh, and the mother! His tattoos mark him as Brigante.

Morcant looks like a wild man in a bloodstained tunic. The wolf, if anyone can see him, is at high alert watching the big warrior. I don't want to think about my own appearance: I can't imagine that I make a good impression.

I greet the leader in the formal language of the tribes. His eyes widen.

'Where have you come from? Isn't that Roman dress?' He surveys my garish, stained and immodest robe with some confusion. 'We don't want any business with collaborators. We're not all in Roman pockets.' His eyes linger on my sword and on Morcant. Morcant may be bedraggled and shoeless, but he's still tall, broad and, with the wolf awake, a fighter. I notice that Morcant has covered his Roman tattoo with mud. I speak before the warrior can say more.

'We've had a bit of trouble. I apologise for our disreputable appearance but we've had to make do with what we could find. Our own gear was stolen, we've come to trade for more.' I pause for a moment and point at my sword. 'But for this we'd have lost our lives too.'

I can see him deliberating. The presence of the sword marks me as either a thief or a warrior and I see him deciding which is the most probable. Oh, by Lugh, he has decided that I'm a thief.

'That's a fine sword you have there. I would trade for that.'

I put my hand on its hilt. I don't know if I would beat him in a fight. He is big and strong but also old and a little above his fighting weight. He would tire easily, but perhaps no more easily than me.

'Ah. It is an heirloom as well as the tool of my trade and I fear that I would grow very hungry and very desperate before I would trade that.' Our eyes lock. I hope he sees in mine my intention to kill him, or die trying, if he were to try to wrest the sword from me. The moment extends as such moments do. I evaluate him as I might an enemy. He does not plant his weight equally; his right side is more muscular than his left. He has one finger missing from his right hand, which will affect his grip.

'You have Roman coin?' It is a backing down of sorts. I am careful not to sigh my relief. From the corner of my eye I see the wolf and the man stand down.

'Ah. Indeed, but as I am of your tribe, I would hope that you will not take advantage of my desperate state but treat me fairly.' I smile, knowing that he'll take advantage. Thank the gods, this is no different to the horse-trading of my father and I do at least know how to haggle.

He allows us into the village itself. The young men stare at me with undisguised wonder. One of them sniggers. I try to muster what dignity I can and hold my head high. The leader, Ger, directs me to a seat outside the largest round-house where a fire struggles to stay alight in the damp air. Morcant squats beside me and tries to look servile. Women are grinding grain for bread. They send me sidelong looks. I feel ridiculous in Cassie's thin stola; my slave brand throbs.

Ger enjoys the game of trading and is much better at it than I am. We settle on a huge sum for some worn-out shoes, well-used clothes and an ancient longsword that is better than it seems. The jewels have been stripped from the hilt and it needs a bit of restoration, but its balance is good and I can see by the patterns in the blade that it was made by a master at his craft.

I am not sure why anyone would trade this, for it is a good fighting blade. I try to keep the question from my eyes. I don't succeed.

'It was my brother's. I have no sons and not even a feisty daughter to carry it in his stead. I would rather trade it than see it go to someone who can't see past a pretty pommel to the quality of the steel.' I nod. Warriors, for all that they dedicate their life to causing mayhem, are among the most sentimental of people and a blade, it is said, has a soul of its own. 'We are as blessed by your generosity as you are blessed by the gods.' He has still done the more favourable deal, as I can tell from Morcant's look of horror, but the trade is not disastrous. I cannot expect Morcant to know about blades. The short stabbing thing he called a gladius was as nothing to this work of craftsmanship.

We seal the deal with a shared meal. There is no way out of that. I feel nervous for no reason that I can explain. Perhaps it is just that I am unused to being with my own people. I glance at Morcant who gives me a reassuring grin. The wolf is still alert in him, and watchful and that makes me feel a little better. The meal will be eaten before full dark, though that is no guarantee that Morcant won't transform.

I'm invited into one of the smaller roundhouses to change my clothes. It smells like my childhood home and reminds me of all the things that I've lost. I swap Cassie's bathhouse wear for good wool, stinking of other people's use but warm and modest. One of the women helps me to dress and makes sure that nothing I have not traded makes its way into my belt pouch. She is more than happy to take the stola. She fingers the fine fabric with near reverence. She'll be lucky to get it clean again after such hard use as I've given it. She smiles at me, showing an untidy row of ill-shaped teeth, and touches my hair, which has started to curl in the dampness. "Tis a pity to lose your glory but it suits you short.' I am touched by her compliment and her warmth: kindness unsettles me now.

The women produce a feast of some quality, better than I'd expected. We sit around the hearth fire of the largest house on an assortment of skins, stools and couches. I sit close to the elderly druid who has the place of honour. That makes me nervous. Druids make me nervous. Children squat close to their mothers and Morcant sits with the other slaves in the chilly place away from the fire. I avoid their eyes.

139

Ger is an expansive host, loud and talkative. I know at once that our arrival is a welcome break from the tedium of winter and Ger intends to make the most of it. I dare not look Morcant's way too often but when I do he seems in control of himself. I am beginning to hope that we might get away without disaster when the druid brings out his harp and makes the customary request that others should join in the entertainment. I feel a chill of foreboding.

I loved this time when I was a child and for a moment I am transported to another fireside and another old druid: my brothers' boasting songs, my mother's haunting lullabies. At Ger's hearth, I am moved when a small girl sings a song of Lugh with a sweet, lisping voice. A young man with hair as red as the Parisi pedlar's sings a drinking song and Ger recounts the story of his most famous battle and then all eyes turn to me. I can sing, of course, it is part of every child's education, but my voice is neither sweet nor strong. I clear my throat, ready to launch into one of the old tunes that everyone knows, but the druid stops me.

'Ah, but music is not your gift, honoured guest. You have another more valuable skill to share with us . . .' It is suddenly very hot and close in the space round the central hearth. The fire blazes a little more wildly and sparks fly. I am aware of the wolf's yellow eyes turning to fix themselves on the old man and of Morcant pausing in the act of drinking. If this

140

turns bad, there is little he can do: little either of us can do. It is bad luck that in this village the druid is one of the gifted. There are enough who are not, clever men and women who learn the lore but have no gods-given talents beyond their wits. I smile and look modest.

'Revered sage, I fear you bestow on me honours I do not deserve, praise I do not merit and expectations I cannot fulfil. My voice is a poor thing it is true, but unless you wish me to fight for my dinner I have little else with which to entertain you.' I was taught to speak this way back home. Big occasions demand fine words and a formal feast, however humble the home, is always a big occasion. I know at once that it's no good. This man's oddly coloured eyes are sharp and he knows what I am. I don't know what other gifts he has but he can recognise a seeress when he sees one. My pulse starts to race.

'But, cariad, is it not true that you are a seeress?' Everyone is staring at me. Everyone stops talking. Mothers hush their babies and even the dogs are quietened. There is no way out. My gift is always an affliction but at moments like this it threatens to become a death sentence. I never see good things and if he makes me touch someone I will almost certainly see things they will not want known. The druid's eyes flash with a golden light. I don't understand why he is making me do this. These are violent times and too many stories will end badly.

'Now, my beauteous seer, do you see the future in entrails, in the smoke of the fire or in the pattern of the stars?'

I'm relieved that he doesn't know everything about me. Perhaps I might lie? Something in his face tells me that wouldn't be wise.

'I have visions,' I mumble in a low voice, but the room has grown so still I might as well have shouted. 'Sometimes I see things if I touch a person's flesh.'

'Come then, honoured guest, touch me.'

There is no getting away from this. All eyes are on me. There is no escape. The druid rules here. I feel Morcant and the wolf willing me to say nothing stupid, but I am powerless. I must tell what I see. My throat is dry and I can feel the tension clenched in the muscles of my belly. The druid's hand is as soft as worn leather. Within that skin his bones are sharp and brittle as dried twigs for the fire. I see the men of fire and steel again. I see the druid burning, his mouth open in a howl of animal agony ... I drop his hand as if I myself had been burned. There is something else too, but I don't want to see it.

I am panting, fighting for calm, unable to get my breath, and I know he reads the horror on my face.

'Tell me, child,' he says and the strange light in his eyes compels me.

'Fire, burning you,' I whisper with my dry throat. 'I think it has something to do with the invaders.'

'Here?'

I shake my head. 'I don't think so. Somewhere else.'

'Is it safe here?' he asks.

I close my eyes. Blood stains the walls, the floor. The round-house is open to the sky. Crows peck at the faces of slaughtered, rotting cattle. 'No!' I say but it is more a sob than a word.

He looks at me for a long time and for a moment I think I see something shadowing him, dark and watchful. Sometimes it is hard to know what is real and what is not. I am trembling all over, quaking with the shock of what I've seen. I wonder what else he will make me do. He seems to come to a decision and turns from me.

'Time for a song, Megan,' he says gaily, as if I had not just foreseen his death. A young woman rises from her seat to entertain, while I sink down to squat beside the druid's feet.

He pats my head as though I were a hound who had pleased him in the hunt. 'Such truths are hard to live with,' he says softly while Megan sings, 'but we all must die and for a druid rebirth must surely follow. I would like to spend time with you and your most interesting companion.' He turns to the place where Morcant sits; the wolf squirms and looks away. Then the druid is focusing on me and I want to run from his gaze. His body may be feeble but his will is powerful. I am afraid of him.

'We can't talk here, but I will see you again. I'm no seer but even I know that. We may help each other before the end, but now it would be best if you leave at once.' He flares his nostrils as though he can smell something unpleasant. 'There is danger for you here. I thank you for the truth you have given me. I will try to stay away from the heat and you should do the same.'

I know that he is trying to warn me of something but I don't know what it is. Megan's voice is strong and true and when the song is over, I praise her talent, the generosity of my hosts and the pleasures of their company. I delight in our shared lineage and promise eternal friendship and then I do as the druid says and get out of there as fast as possible. Morcant, watching my every breath, is ahead of me, slinking through the doorway like a chastised dog. The wolf's ears are flat against his head. The old warrior, Ger, seems puzzled by my haste. I am not surprised when he follows me out a few moments later to say his own farewell.

'I'm not a bearer of good news,' I say in answer to his unspoken question. 'The gods bless me with knowledge of their darker intentions. I thank you for the sword and I pray that I use it well on both our enemies.'

'Be careful,' he says, 'not everyone here is loyal to our tribe. Wait!' He disappears for a moment and returns pulling an old mare. 'The druid says you are working for the tribes, that you stand with us.' He looks uncomfortable. 'He asked me to give you this.' He removes one of his own golden arm rings and gives it to me. The ring is broad as the width of my hand and thick as my thumbnail is long. It is a gift of great price.

'I can't take this!'

'It was never mine. It's druid-made, brought from the Sacred Isle, from Mona. I am told it brings certain blessings on the right people.' He sighs. 'Not me. The druid says you need it – it will help you to see more clearly.'

I take the arm ring from his callused hands, taking care not to touch him. I like this old warrior and I don't want images of his death to haunt me. I slide it on to my forearm and, lacking Ger's bulky muscle, have to push it up to my upper arm. He tightens it with the pressure of his meaty hand. If he notices my brand, he chooses to ignore it.

'If you are seeking Caratacus, keep travelling west and be careful of who you trust. There is a lot of double-dealing going on. It is a long way and you may have need of Mari, here.'

I take the mare's halter. I start to thank Ger but he waves my gratitude away. 'You will pay if you fight the fight for us. May the goddess bless you and Taranis keep you.' He clasps my arm, warrior to warrior. I can't avoid the contact and I am grateful that I do not see his death with that touch. Instead, I see a baby in the arms of his wife, Bethan, the woman who admired my hair. I cannot help smiling at such a rare, joyous vision.

'You might get yourself an heir, yet,' I say, 'and when you do, I'll be happy to return your sword.'

He shrugs and I know he doesn't believe me; he gave up that hope long ago.

Morcant waits for him to return indoors before emerging from the shadows. Something in his stance tells me he is not happy.

'Are you all right?'

He nods. 'You?' he croaks.

'The druid – I don't know ... he described you as my "most interesting companion". Do you think he knows?'

Morcant doesn't answer. Then I hear the she-wolf's lonely call and I understand. He is struggling to listen to me. The wolf is howling in response.

'Go,' I say. He needs no further urging. 'I'm still heading west,' I shout after him. He doesn't need to know that, but it helps me to say it. It makes it seem as if we have an agreement, that we have arranged to meet again. I watch as he runs ahead along the darkening cart track and then beyond towards the forest. He is the beast again, the great shadow wolf re-formed into dense flesh and solid muscle. He is hard to spot, he moves so swiftly, a blur of darkness deeper than the dusk. It is not a betrayal. I know it's not a betrayal but I feel very alone.

I collect Morcant's discarded clothes, fold them as if I

were his mother and stow them along with the sword on Mari's back. I mount her and kick my heels into the flanks of the placid mare and she obediently breaks into a trot. The sun dips behind the trees and I slip into the forest yet again like a swimmer breaking the surface of a fathomless pool and all around me the night shades flow.

CHAPTER TWENTY

Morcant's Story

The she-wolf is close and howling. I can smell her and her scent alone is enough to raise the wolf in me. This time I know the transformation is coming and I run. I have to make it to the shelter of the trees, out of sight of the tribespeople and the old druid. I should stay with Trista but I can't; the she-wolf needs me and her call is urgent and demanding and my nature responds. I can feel the pull of my other self, my other life. The darkness pulses with the heartbeats of our potential prey. I can taste the night on my tongue; too many flavours, too many scents; the richness of it all confuses me and I need the she-wolf. She shows me and leads me and teaches me the ways of our kind. I feel so much energy and power that I want to run and never stop, run away from the midden of the village and the stench of fear. She waits for me, in plain sight, in the clearing. I race towards her as a man, clumsy and awkward. She fixes me with her keen eyes and stays her ground. She is poised ready to flee, but she does not. She knows me by scent and waits for the inevitable. By the time I reach her I am a wolf and free. No more words. Just the night.

CHAPTER TWENTY-ONE

Trista's Story

I try not to be irritated by Morcant's transformation, but I am. I hate these nights in the forest. The forest is full of shadows, flickering images glimpsed at the edge of my vision. Tonight the shadows are thickening, taking form, as clear as Morcant's spectral wolf. Over there an old giant, gnarled as ancient wood, sits in an oak tree watching me and here, ghostly as mist, strange creatures skulk in the long grass. I pretend I've not seen them. It grows dark quickly. There is no cloud and the night is icily bright; the moon's light is cold as frost.

It is possible that I am descending into madness. I feel as though a thousand eyes survey my every move. I ride with one hand resting on my sword – as if that will help.

I'm too afraid to stop. A triple-headed woman, pale as sap, sits on a tree branch and combs her hair of twigs. I mumble my prayer to her but she just keeps combing her hair with razored hands. I hum snatches of sacred songs, mutter invocations and flattery to the wraiths and divinities that haunt this place, beg help of any who might have an interest in my protection. Clenched within my guts is a tight fist of fear.

My eyes are gritty with fatigue when Morcant and the she-wolf finally appear, almost hidden by the undergrowth, in the shadows of the trees. Morcant the wolf turns towards me and there is that strange smearing of form, as if the village painter has smudged his image on the hall wall, then the huge shaggy outline of the grey wolf shrinks to become the man, Morcant, who kneels on his hands and knees, naked in the mud of the forest floor. The she-wolf holds her ground even as a wolf becomes a man. If it's strange for me, how much stranger it must be for her. I see her tense, her tail and ears drop, then Morcant reaches out his hand to stroke her tawny head and she licks his fingers as if she were an ordinary hound. Morcant puts his face next to hers and she licks that too. His knees are visibly trembling as he hauls himself up on to two legs, his feet are splayed at a strange angle as if he has forgotten how to balance on two legs and he has to use the sturdy she-wolf to right himself. The relationship between them is so trusting and intimate that I feel uncomfortable observing them. I don't say anything as he staggers towards me.

Ever practical I dismount and hand over his clothes. 'See anything useful on your travels?' I ask.

He shakes his head and scratches the stubble on his chin; he does it as a dog might scratch his neck. I wonder if with each transformation he becomes a little less human.

'There are man tracks everywhere in the forest – some old, some new. We stayed away from all of them.' He shrugs as he struggles into his tunic. His pale torso is criss-crossed by small cuts and abrasions, marks of the wolf's history on his human flesh. I find myself staring at his well-muscled bare chest and have to force myself to look away. Ger had stowed a bag of bread on the mule and I offer Morcant some. He eats it greedily, from which I gather that his hunting last night was not a success.

'Trista?' He struggles to get the word out.

'What?'

'The wolf is getting stronger.'

I thought he looked bigger and fitter than before, then I realise that isn't what he means.

'You're stronger too.' Even as a man he seems more powerful. The strain of my night's visions has made me so weary, I can barely speak. I have to rest, if only for a short while. I attend to the mare. Morcant keeps his distance. 'I've been riding all night – would you be able to stand watch for a while?'

He hesitates and seems about to speak, but my eyes are already closing.

I wake with a start I don't know how much time later. The sun is high. I am freezing and Morcant is gone.

It takes me a moment to stand up. My feet are numb. The things I saw last night are still lurking in the undergrowth, creatures of mist or madness. I rub my eyes but they still remain. I think I hear something and the creatures scatter like birds in a battle. Someone is coming and Morcant has abandoned me. I stagger after my lost mare. Fortunately she hasn't wandered far away. Was the food I ate in Ger's hall poisoned or cursed? My body feels as slow as my brain.

I ride for a while before I see him, all but hidden in the gloom of the forest. He is a beast again. He carries something bloody in his mouth. I think it's a rabbit. He looks as embarrassed as a wolf can. The shadow man that is his human self will not meet my eye.

'You should not have left me!' I sound aggrieved, like a nagging wife, even though I'm right. I can see the she-wolf behind him, eyeing me warily. She is still a wild creature. She sniffs the air, glances at Morcant, then turns and runs. I think Morcant is about to do the same; he turns as if to follow her but then stops. He watches me, waits for me. I urge the mare further into the wood, following the she-wolf. Whatever is a threat to the wolves will surely be a threat to me.

The half-seen things that seem to live here are all heading

153

in the same direction, away from the source of the noise I thought I'd heard. They crawl and limp, flutter past my ear on crooked wings or swing from the winter trees. Morcant walks alongside me, keeping his distance from the mare but matching his pace to hers. We go as quickly as I dare but the ground is treacherous and carpeted with a heaving crowd of eldritch beings. Luckily the mare doesn't seem to notice.

There is no doubt now. I can hear voices. I don't want to be caught defenceless and fleeing.

I halt the mare and slide from her back. I waste moments struggling into my mail. It is difficult enough even when my hands aren't stiff with cold. I need help that Morcant's paws can't give me. Finally I manage to pull it down over my hips, belt my sword and grab my helmet. It has taken me too long; the voices are getting closer. I make for Morcant's side.

Morcant begins to run, but slowly so I can keep up in my heavy shirt and poor condition. They are gaining on us. I don't know how many there are but it sounds like more than we can fight. They are speaking the Roman tongue. I'm getting to recognise it even though I still cannot tell one word from another. Morcant the wolf bares his teeth. Morcant the shadow man reaches out as if to touch my hand. His spectral fingers hover over mine. His keen senses will have told him exactly how many men pursue us: he thinks it's over for us. I try to run faster but my legs have nothing left to give. I stumble and only save myself by falling on the wolf. I turn to see the twenty or so armed men stride into view. I draw my sword. We can't fight so many but I'm ready to die trying. I glance towards Morcant who bares his teeth. At least the she-wolf got away.

A hail of spears lands close to me. Morcant growls and backs away. He does not run, even though he would be too fast for these men to capture or kill. He should save himself. Do they know who we are? Do they think us the thieves, deserters, murderers who escaped the fort of the Ninth Legion?

They have come prepared. Three men approach with spears and a net of the kind we use for fishing. It seems that they do know who we are. I grip my sword more tightly, ready to back Morcant when he attacks, but as the men come closer he does the last thing I expect. He allows them to take him: a weaker wolf will always submit to the stronger.

They hang him from a pole like a slaughtered boar, or a deer, like meat hunted for a feast. I have rarely felt so help-less. I cannot run and I cannot fight. All I can do is endure.

A tall man with the fair skin of a northman approaches me. I sheathe my sword. My chances of getting away were slim with Morcant; they don't exist without him. There is nothing to be gained from fighting this one man. He is tall, fit and rested, and there are too many more. He is speaking at me, making harsh guttural sounds which mean less than

Morcant's growls. He grabs my helmet, pulls it roughly from my head and hits me – an open-handed slap across my face. The blow stings and I taste blood where his ring breaks my skin. I've been in this position before. I can't bear it again. I hang my head, not in shame but in a kind of weariness. I am already broken: bereaved, abandoned, beset by visions and delusions, lost. There is no need to break me further.

The northman shoves me towards the rest of the men. They are all in armour, except for one – a young red-headed man dressed as a tribesman. At first I think it is the Parisi pedlar because his face is familiar, but then I realise it is one of Ger's men, the one who sang a drinking song. He must have left before me and ridden hard to bring a detachment after me so swiftly. I ought to have taken more notice of the druid's and Ger's warnings. Did they guess they had a Roman sympathiser in their midst?

He pulls my head back upright, by my hair. 'Seeress slut,' he says in my own language. He is not gentle and I want to spit in his face, but I don't. Perhaps in this I have to follow the wolf. I have reverted to the slave, Trista, who somehow survived when it might have been more honourable to die.

What frightens me most is the sudden return of my visions. The last thing I need right now is to be lost in some other now, when I need my wits about me. Someone punches me in the guts for no particular reason and I pitch forward, hunched around the site of the assault. Perhaps I should have made a stand but someone slices through my sword belt and takes my weapon before I can launch a belated attack. I see the sword with a plunderer's eye, the elaborate designs on the leather sheath; its jewelled hilt set in gold is a prize to be fought for. It causes me almost physical pain to see it taken from me: I have never carried a finer blade.

CHAPTER TWENTY-TWO

Trista's Story

I keep my head down for all of the day's march. I don't know where they are taking us both or why. I don't understand why we haven't been killed at once.

I find out when the young Kelt chooses to taunt me.

'This lot make sacrifices to their she-wolf god who founded their city. Their festival Lupercalia is tonight. You and your wolf are going to die, unnatural bitch. They don't like women pretending to be men, especially Roman men. They're going to make you suffer!'

My throat is dry or I might be tempted to curse him. I don't understand why he is taking such pleasure in this. I don't understand. It doesn't help that I can still see phantoms wherever I look. Even the northman's hard slap hasn't knocked any sense into me.

I try to twist so that I can see Morcant and gauge how he takes this news, but I get another slap for my trouble. The grey creatures watch, apparently unmoved. I have finally worked out who they are: the Wild Weird who lived in this land before all else. I still don't know why I am able to see them, but it is possible that they too are real.

I walk at the same steady pace as the soldiers. The rhythm of it, not quite a march nor yet a shamble, begins to act as a chant or a ritual drumbeat. The jangle of the soldiers' belts, the slap of their feet on the mud lull me into a trance, take me to that other place where visions come. I think I moan and once I know I cry out: all I see are images of death and burning as if the whole of this vast land is ablaze and every warrior in it, fighting to the death. Even the grey creatures are dying, melting away with each tribal death.

I think the commander is worried about me. Someone feels my forehead which burns as if with fever. Someone lets me sit and drink a little watered wine. I dare not take too much as I know it will only make things worse. Wine always loosens the stretched threads that anchor me to the here and now. Someone unties Morcant too, though they have muzzled and tethered him. A live sacrifice kept fit and whole until death is likely to suffer greatly and increase the power of the offering. I think I might be sick.

While we rest, the soldiers build a fire and start to cook their evening meal. They send the Keltic traitor to ask me if I need anything. I refuse to speak. Something has happened to my loyalties, something I didn't expect: the Romans have become my enemy. I don't want the Romans to do to Ger's clan what they did to the Chief's hall. I was raised as a Brigante warrior. I will fight for my tribe against its enemies. The Romans have just become my tribal enemies and I will fight against Rome itself if I have to.

My visions cease once we stop marching. My head clears. I'm not going to walk to my death like a sheep to the butcher's knife. I've done with slavery and dumb acceptance of my fate. I was wrong. I'm not yet broken, only dangerously cracked. There has to be a way to escape. I have to reclaim my sword, my sword belt and my pouch with that scratched bark for Caratacus.

I can't do much but sit for a while. The smells of cooking make me weak with hunger and I don't have the strength to turn down food when it is offered. It is only then, when my belly is full, that I notice Morcant sniffing the air, tense and wary. His human shadow is as alert as the wolf. Something is coming. Morcant the spectral man meets my eyes and signals. I will be ready.

The Romans have left my hands unbound. They might well regret that.

I mime that I need to relieve myself. The soldier guarding me leers and makes some remarks I'm glad I don't understand, but the northman gives permission. I am surrounded by armed men – what can I do? I lower my eyes and walk like I'm a slave again. These men are all used to ignoring those who serve them as I am – or was. I round my shoulders, hide my height, shuffle as though the fight has been beaten out of me. I stumble into a soldier cleaning his sword. He grunts and says something I'm pretty sure is obscene. I allow him to hit me with the flat of his gladius. I moan a bit to make him know how much it hurts. It stings and I will have a bruise there if I live to see tomorrow. I endured worse every day in training as a girl. The pain focuses my mind. It reminds me that I'm not dead yet. I have lost fitness in the months of slavery, but I'm still quick as a bird. These Romans wear their pugio so obviously they almost invite theft. This blade is not as fine as the last one I purloined, but it will serve me well enough. The legionary doesn't notice. I slide it up my arm, hiding it inside the sleeve of my tunic, and when he is done with his yelling and beating, I shuffle awkwardly away.

I disappear behind a tree to reorder my dress so that the pugio is hidden under my cloak. The wolf is tethered away from the fire – he would put anyone off their food. He is enormous. I can see that he is doing his best to look like a beaten dog; his head rests on his paws as hounds lie at their master's feet. I need a diversion.

The fire is always in me and it is easy to make the cook fire blaze and spit. The men round the fire leap back, a cloak catches and they have to beat it out. The flames are high as a man's shoulder. They withdraw in panic and in their conversations I hear words that sound like curses. While they argue over what has caused the problem and how to fix it, I wander over towards the wolf and slice through the hemp rope that binds him. He licks my hand and I scratch the fur behind his ears.

I can tell by the wolf's eagerness that whatever is coming is nearly with us. We must be ready. He gets unsteadily to his feet. The Romans have hurt him. I run my hands over his back; there is no blood but the awkward way they carried him must have pulled muscles and ligaments. His tail and ears are down. There is nothing I can do to help him.

'It'll be all right,' I whisper to him in my own language. Somehow both of us have temporarily forgotten the men who are our captors. The northman sees me standing with the liberated wolf and yells something. His men grab spears and I know that we must run. There is no need to speak. We are of one mind in this – we run for the treeline as fast as our various injuries allow.

My side feels as if a spear has pierced it, though I know that it is only the after-effects of the beating I was given. Still I run. The steady smack of feet tells me that the men are not far behind. The wolf has stopped. Could it be that he waits for me? I am gasping, my chest is heaving, my lungs are on fire. I wish I could make sense of the Romans' language, for the air is thick with commands and it would help if I could understand what is going on. The wolf looks at me. His eyes glimmer in the darkness like steel. I rest my hand on his head. Is it time to stand? For the first time I notice how the grey folk surround Morcant the shadow man. He speaks to them and it looks to my incredulous eyes as if they understand. They turn as I turn to face the men running towards us. I stand knee-deep in an army of shadows. Their presence chills my bones. I don't know what harm they can do to the bulky well-armed men who, even in the gathering darkness, are so much more real than these phantoms of smoke and air.

I remove my hand from Morcant's head, raise my stolen dagger and yell: 'Charge!' as if it were my war cry. The sound rings out and releases us both. Morcant leaps. He is a blur of bunched muscle, of raw power. He hurls himself at the first of the legionaries, knocking him to the ground. The gladius falls from the man's hand. Someone screams. A man wields a blazing brand stolen from the fire as if it were a weapon, but a grey snake with human arms launches itself at him, winding its body around the man's throat so that for a moment his eyes bulge and he seems to gasp for air. The brand falls to the ground and everyone is yelling at once. The power of the grey people is limited but they distract and disrupt and in battle any small advantage can be made to count. I scrabble for the sword, darting quickly between the feet of my enemy. I duck an ill-timed, half-hearted blow because everyone is looking at Morcant. My own eyes are fixed on my enemy. A man screams in agony as I hear Morcant's growl, and I have to guess the rest. From the corner of my eye I see the wolf's open maw ripping at the man's throat. Blood sprays. Men who should be able to best me are backing out of my way and a tide of the shadow creatures are with me, entangling the legs of my enemy, creating chaos and confusion.

Distantly I hear the she-wolf howl. Not now. Why can't she leave him alone? He cannot afford the distraction. Morcant stops mid-stride, throws back his huge head and howls a response. It echoes and for a moment it is all that there is in the whole world.

All other sounds cease, rendered meaningless by the primal power of his voice; there is only the beast and his mate filling the night with their haunting, marrow-chilling cry. The men watch him in a kind of awe. He is the biggest wolf I have ever seen and his cry lifts the hairs on my neck and chills my blood – and he and I are allies. The men watch, their eyes wide. Morcant is a creature of legend.

The awe does not last for long. These Romans are not much given to it. A spear misses Morcant by less than a hair's breadth. The men are responding to commands now in better order and our feeble chances of survival diminish further. I pray more earnestly than I have ever prayed before to the local gods to add their power to that of their minions.

I drop into a fighting stance. I could wish for a better sword than this gladius and a few more warriors beside me but there is a kind of freedom in knowing that I cannot survive. There is liberation in knowing that all I need do is fight for my honour as a warrior and reduce the ranks of my enemies by as many men as I can. I sing out my ululating war cry and there is a kind of joy in it. There is no dishonour in such an end – even Gwyn would admit that.

Most of the men have mustered so quickly that they've left their shields behind at the fireside. Without shields battle with a gladius is an intimate affair. I can feel the heat of their bodies in the chill of the night, smell their sweat. The reach of the gladius is so short that to stab them with it, I must move in close, as if for an embrace. My first attacker is a dark-eyed, dark-skinned man from somewhere far from here. I go in for a low and vicious blow. I am quick and strong. I watch his dark eyes widen with surprise then turn glassy as I send him to a still further place. I have to pull hard to free the gladius from his flesh. I ask a silent blessing on his soul and then step over him to meet the next foe: a tall warrior with the freckled look of a tribesman. I take a deep breath to steady myself. The Wild Weird are clustering around me, tugging at me, urging me – to do what? I exhale and my breath is fire. It is as if I have become a dragon of legend. It gushes out of me as though I am a blazing torch. The yellow tongues of flame lick my enemy's face, his mail, his sword, hungry and eager to consume him whole. The heat singes the ends of my hair, blisters my throat and burns my teeth. My opponent screams a raw, desperate sound. He retreats, enveloped in flame, burning.

I take my place beside the beast. I abandon all thoughts of fighting hand-to-hand and set fire to everything that I can. No one dares approach us. The men are too busy stamping to put out the fire that consumes their cloaks, that catches their hair, that makes the clearing suddenly blaze with light and flames. The grey creatures, almost indistinguishable now from the dark smoke that billows on the wind, rush to fan the flames. Was it their power or my own that made that deadly flame?

The Romans are admirable in their way – so well-drilled they help each other and the tactic does not buy us as much time as I'd hoped. My lips are blistered. My face feels raw and scorched. The pain in my throat is hard to bear: I don't think I can try this again.

Morcant is panting. His solid muscular flanks pulse with his breath. His open mouth frightens me; his teeth are so large and sharp. Neither the man nor the wolf seem likely to submit this time. I feel a sudden wave of regret, sharp and sweet at once. I wish that I had time to know him better. I wish that I could have paid my debt to Cassie; a seeress should keep her word.

As I had expected some of the men have run behind us to encircle us – an obvious tactic when they are so many and we are so few. Morcant presses his flank against my leg as close to me as he can get. He turns his huge head to look at me, and I find myself smiling. The man and the beast are one to me now: my friend.

Morcant snarls again and swipes the air with his tail. He leaves my side and paces out a tight circle, facing each of our enemies in turn, giving them the chance to see the size of his teeth, his claws, the strength contained in the taut muscles rippling under that thick covering of fur. All of them, to a man, take a step backwards. Those that had spears appear to have thrown them. I think we can thank the spoiling tactics of the grey folk for the Romans' unusually poor aim. Without their shields the legionaries will have to move in close for the kill, close enough to feel the sharpness of Morcant's teeth, to feel the thrust of my stolen sword tear through unprotected flesh, spilling the softer parts within. Some of them will die. This impasse lasts for no more than five rapid heartbeats, but it is all the time I need to say my goodbyes and pray to the gods that I might die a good death and find a good rebirth when my time with the shades of the dead is over.

I try to scream out my war cry from my parched throat. Nothing much happens and it feels like my throat is tearing. The northman finally finds his voice, gives an order and they step forward all together, one pace only. The human net around us is tightening. Morcant is ready to pounce and I am poised to pierce the lad closest to me. He is nearly my age and I can almost taste his fear. Something is wrong though – there is a disturbance and men are suddenly shouting. I do not take my eyes off the man I have chosen as my victim. I move forward thrusting and stabbing with my borrowed sword, putting all my weight and power into it. I should be assailed by weapons as my blade finds yielding flesh, but my victim's comrades have turned away; the circle that surrounds us falls apart. My man falls. I hear a wild ululating tribesman's cry. Could it be that we have reinforcements? Morcant is fighting two men, a blur of grey fur. Around him men scatter and behind them I see them: Ger and the men from the village.

The legionaries do what they can to fall back to the camp-fire to regroup. The first casualty is my betrayer, the man from Ger's own village, who falls to the ground, a tribal spear through his chest.

Ger is impressive with his hair limed so that it stands up, giving him an extra span of height. The gold torque around his thick neck is polished and glinting in the torchlight. He runs to my side. I want to smile but my burned lips hurt too much.

'Are you all right? I feared we'd be too late.'

I nod. I'm not all right but I am alive. Once more, just as I am ready to die, I am given another chance. I fight the urge to embrace Ger. I am so overwhelmed. He has saved me. My raw throat seizes up and I struggle to get any words out at all. I want to tell him not to attack the wolf. I look around for Morcant but he has gone. Ger shouts his orders and a young boy helps me towards the back of the horde while Ger engages my enemies. The boy gives me water from his canteen.

'The Lord Druid said we had to move quickly to save you. You are the hope of the tribes!' I don't know what he is talking about. 'Once we worked out that Madoc had gone we mustered at once and Ma and the women have abandoned the village because of your warning.' As he talks his eyes dart from one man to the next, watching, straining to join in. I put my hand on his arm to stop him running into the thick of the fighting. I want to cover his ears so that he doesn't have to hear the cries, the butcher sounds of metal hacking bone, but he is of age or Ger would not have brought him. I am glad to rest away from the fighting. I've done enough killing. Ger has brought more than twenty men and the Romans are down to five, two of whom are quite badly burned. There is only one way this will go.

The Romans did not have time enough to get themselves into good battle order. They fight bravely and well but they are no match for the joyous madness of Ger and his men. The boy almost wriggles away.

'This is not your time,' I say, as if I've seen his future. I am glad to say I have not, but he's in such awe of me he leaves the killing to his elders.

My throat is agonisingly raw. I want to follow Morcant except that I know that he's gone where I cannot follow. My eyes burn and I do not realise for quite some time that they are blurred less from the smoke than from my tears. I am alive and abandoned by the only companion I want; Morcant has gone back to his she-wolf.

CHAPTER TWENTY-THREE

Trista's Story

I am exhausted and I give myself up to the visions. There is little to choose between the scene before me and the pictures I see with my mind's eye: people are dying in both.

I'm brought back to myself by the homely scent of ale and the savoury smell of bread.

'Trista?' Ger shakes me gently. When I open my eyes, it is his gap-toothed smile I see.

'We won, my girl. You did well to fight them off for so long. You're safe now.'

Can I ever be safe? The sun is high in a pale blue sky. I am lying under a thick plaid blanket and there are no trees to be seen. There are no bodies either. I sit up and accept the beaker of ale and hunk of bread from Ger's hand.

'Whaa?' I begin. It is a sound not a word and it hurts to make even such a sound. I go to wipe my mouth and find it smeared with sticky ointments. Every part of me aches and I am stiff from the beating at the legionaries' hands. I don't think I've been cut, but it is hard to tell.

'You were out of it, girl, so after we'd done what was needed we put you on your horse and brought you here.' Now I can see it is a tribal encampment with people and livestock all corralled together in a temporary stockade. A huge central hearth has been built and the women are roasting what looks like venison on a spit. The smell of burning meat is too close to the stench of burning flesh. It makes my stomach heave.

'Our Lord Druid took your words to heart and has taken himself off to find Caratacus. It was decided that we shall all follow his lead and offer ourselves to his service. Those that want to throw their lot in with Rome can follow Madoc's path and risk his fate. Whatever our Queen has to say about it, I'll not give my crops to Roman masters.' He looks angry but then he looks at me and his brow clears. 'There is no need for you to risk the road alone. I think we were wrong to send you on your way with no one but a slave. We are all in this together now. It will take us a while as we have brought all we can carry with us.' He waves his hand to encompass the village of crude shelters.

I feel responsible. Was it my vision that did this? I think he must see that thought flit across my face. 'The wind has been blowing this way for a while, girl. I've had a few visits from the armed men of the legion and I don't like the way they eyed my land. I can't hold what is mine against the legions. I might be old but I'm not stupid.'

I nod. I try to speak but nothing but a croak comes out of my dry throat so I drink the spiced ale instead and remember the night of my escape from the hall when I would have given almost anything to taste its flavour again: it was worth the wait.

'We found your gear: the mare, your sword and mine, oh, and this.' He hands me the pouch with the message for Caratacus still intact inside it. 'Not much of a one for keeping hold of things, are you?'

I'm about to try to explain but he puts his hand over mine. 'I'm joking with you. You did well to survive. You're truly worthy of this blade.' He presses my longsword into my hand. As my fingers curl around it I can't help but smile. The tiny movement hurts as if the skin around my mouth has shrunk. I still can't speak so I pat his hand in thanks, but my eyes are already beginning to close. Too late I detect the bitterness of a sleeping draught in the aftertaste of the ale.

The next nights pass in a haze. I have visions. I eat. I sleep. I have to trust Ger and I do. His wife, Bethan, spoons warm milk sweetened with honey into my mouth. I know she has laced it with a potion to make me sleep but I don't make a fuss. I'm not allowed to be awake for long. I know they believe that sleep is good for me and so it would be unkind to tell them about the endless horror of my prophetic visions. They are good people and are trying to spare me agony. We travel all day and sometimes for half the night and I am never left untended for very long.

The moon is a waning crescent. I calculate that I have been allowed to rest for almost fifteen nights. Tonight Bethan gives me unadulterated ale, instead of honeyed milk. I'm very weak, but I can swallow without pain.

'So,' Ger begins, 'you are well again.' I nod and cough. I have to force my voice to work after so long a rest.

'I must thank you and your wife for caring for me.'

He grins and opens his arms to include all his gathered clan. 'We have all cared for you as if you are our only child. You have not been the quietest of patients.' There is a low wave of laughter swiftly suppressed. The people at the fire all look at me with such affection I wonder for a moment if I have turned into someone else.

His wife shushes him gently. Perhaps I made more noise than I remember. 'What we all want to know,' she says with a wicked little smile of her own, 'is who is Morcant?'

At his name my body tenses. How can I have forgotten him? Where is he? I think my expression must have changed because she looks penitent at once. 'Oh Trista, I'm sorry. Have I upset you?'

'No, no, it's fine. He is a friend, but we have parted company.' My voice is still husky from lack of use. I try to smile. Has Morcant abandoned me or have I abandoned him?

It is a long time since I've been part of a clan such as this. I don't belong here among this kindly throng of warriors and their wives. I am a warrior, a seeress and now a messenger with a blood debt to repay. I belong with other outcasts. I belong with Morcant.

I watch the leaping flames of the hearth fire for a long time, ignoring the cavorting of the Wild Weird and listening to the sounds of the sleeping tribe. I cannot stay. I wait for the first hint of dawn and then I get ready. I take only what is mine: mail, helmet, sword belt, sword and cloak. I am quiet as I can be, though my legs shake a little from lack of use.

'Wait! You'll need food for your journey,' Bethan whispers to me across the sleeping form of her husband. She gets to her feet.

'I'll see you past the watch.'

She doesn't ask me anything. She is swiftly on her feet gathering up a few small loaves of flatbread into a bag along with some dried venison. She hands me a spear too – one of ours – decorated with interwoven charms, curses and blessings.

'Don't think me ungrateful . . .' I still find it difficult to speak.

She touches my cheek gently; her hands are rough as a

slave's. 'You are not like us. We all know of the horrors that haunt your dreams.' I see her snaggle-toothed smile in the fire-light. I was obviously not as close-mouthed as I might have hoped in all my endless dreaming. 'Our Lord Druid told us to take care of you and we have. Please take care of yourself.'

I hug her as warmly as if she were Cerys. 'May the gods bless you,' I say. 'Say goodbye to Ger. I've left his sword.'

'I hope you find him, your Morcant, and I hope he knows what a prize he has in you.'

She kisses me lightly on the cheek and returns to the fire. Two of the Wild Weird follow her, the rest come with me. I am still puzzling over her words when day breaks.

CHAPTER TWENTY-FOUR

Trista's Story

I feel as if my legs belong to a newly born lamb. I have to lean hard on my spear and wonder if that is why thoughtful Bethan gave it to me. Somehow I breathe better away from all those tribespeople. I am better off alone. That is not true: I am better off with Morcant. I could have stayed with Ger and still fulfilled my debt to Cassie. Bethan understood me well. My leaving Ger's clan is less about Caratacus than about Morcant.

I won't find Morcant on Ger's chosen roads – on the old market tracks. If I want to find the wolf, I'll have to travel through the wilderness, through the forests and the scrublands on the route west. If Morcant is still heading towards Mona, then that will be his path too. The Sabrina and the Sacred Isle are both west of here.

I should have borrowed a horse. I haven't been walking long when I realise that my decision to walk alone through

rough terrain without companionship is more insane than merely foolish. I am weary before the sun has moved in the sky. The Wild Weird are so numerous here I can barely see the ground. Most of them are so terrifying in appearance that I have to avert my eyes. I sing to distract myself, like a mad woman. My voice sounds rusty as an abandoned sword, ugly as a cry of pain.

I keep the sun at my back and pick my way through the dense forest. Sometimes it feels as if the Wild Weird are guiding me, herding me even. That is the trouble with being alone – fancies can become convictions all too easily.

I have to stop to rest, sooner than I'd like. I settle down to eat something and rest against the trunk of an oak tree. It is only then that I see it: a clear pathway lit by a wan, unearthly light that has nothing to do with the weak sun. It is so obvious it could be painted on the ground. The grass is faintly silvered as if rimed with frost and the mud glows with a soft inner fire. I shiver. I know what this is and it is something I never thought to see – the druids' walk, the sacred path, the highway of the dead.

I'm sure now that the Wild Weird have been pushing me in this direction. What would happen if I were to walk that path? I know nothing of the mysteries, the ancient wisdom that might guide me. I've learned enough lore to recognise that the Wild Weird are unreliable allies and they could be urging me to my death. As I wrap my cloak more tightly around my shoulders, my fingers brush against the metal of Ger's arm ring. I'd forgotten all about it. I work it down my arm to take a better look at it in daylight. Now I can see that it is far from being the plain gold band I thought at first. It is very finely wrought, of the most precious rose-hued gold, chased into intricate interlocking patterns; indeed, it is the most beautiful thing I have ever seen. Didn't Ger say it would grant me clear sight? I need that now more than ever before.

I struggle to my feet, using the tree trunk for support. My legs still tremble after any kind of muscular effort. I stumble, right myself, but the precious arm ring rolls from my grasp. It hasn't rolled far. It lies in that section of the ground that was illumined by eldritch light, but now there is no light, no path and no grey folk cavorting at my feet: there is nothing but the dark wood and an eerie silence broken only by my loudly beating heart. I don't know how I failed to grasp the obvious truth. It was not madness or my prophetic power that let me see the grey folk and the druids' walk: it was Ger's gift, that is the clear sight that Ger's druid granted me.

I pick the arm ring up with more care and reverence than I bestowed on it before. As soon as I touch it the path beneath my feet flares into brightness like a pale flame and a swarm of grey folk are gathered round my feet. I push Ger's arm ring higher up my arm and tighten it so that it will not work its way loose. It was a great and terrifying gift that he gave me. Did the druid intend me to walk the druids' walk?

I can't help but rest my hand on my sword as I start my journey again. As soon as I place one foot on the path, the world beyond it dissolves into a blur of greens and greys. I pray that this is the right decision and take a step.

I am somewhere else. Here I am in the summer country. It is warm and the light is golden so that the grass and trees along the way glow like gems: the green of emeralds, the brown of amber, while the path itself has a dazzling diamond glitter. I have seen this place in visions. I want to run from its strangeness and at the same time I never want to leave.

The sound of running water draws me. It is a kind of music in all the quietness. I'm thirsty but I don't drink. I have shown myself to be witless all too often recently but I'm not that much of a fool.

All the trees here are oaks and when I look around me I find that my escort of grey creatures has disappeared. I see the reason at once. Among the trees are seven carved statues, faceless and eyeless – the guardians of this place. At the feet of the nearest carved god I can see the yellowing bone of a human skull stripped bare of flesh, nestling there along with a crown of mistletoe. This is a sacred grove used by the druids. I feel the hairs on my arm stand on end as if I am watched. The statues do not move, but I can feel the life in them. It is a silent pulse, a motionless breath, a vibration in the air: an immanence. It is hard to say what is that intangible difference between the faces of the living and the dead, but everyone knows it when they see it. I see it now. These statues live and the beings within them are ancient and demanding. I am in the presence of a great and terrible power. The statues want something from me and I don't know what. Their nature demands sacrifice – why else would they be present at this place of sacrifice? They wait. The air is heavy with an awful expectation. It is hard even to breathe here. It is as if a physical weight presses against my chest, suffocating me. I can't speak. I'm no druid; I know no charms to beguile these waiting ones, no clever words or incantations. I have few choices. It is the decision of a moment. I draw my sword and kneel at the foot of the largest statue. The green moss that grows there is soft under my knees, like a cushion made to bear the precious flesh of offerings. I don't hesitate. To hesitate would be to falter and to falter would be to fail. I raise my sword and slice across my palm with its razor edge. It is a clean cut, a thin skein of scarlet yarn, a minute crack in the fabric of myself. The pain is sharp. The blood wells dark against my white hand. I lie down at the foot of the tree so that the blood drips into the greedy ground and wait.

I wait for some sign that this might be enough, that they don't want all that I am. I don't listen with my ears but with that other inner part, the part that sees visions and knows what ought to be unknowable. I strain, focused on what I cannot hear and what, even with Ger's gift, I will never see. I wait. What more do they want of me?

I don't know how long I lie there, prostrate on the ground, along with the skeletal remains of other, earlier sacrifices. It happens as slowly as my blood drips, develops like a distant song that grows ever clearer and louder and more joyous. I barely noticed it building, but now it has come I am overwhelmed by an unexpected feeling of wellbeing, an inner warmth surging through me. It is enough. I have done enough. They are satisfied. I cut a strip of cloth from the bottom of my tunic, bind up my hand and heave myself back to standing. There is barely time for any feelings of relief for I am left with the most terrible thirst and an uncontrollable urge to drink from the clear water that flows through the sacred grove.

I stagger towards the bank on legs that seem more unwilling than ever to do my bidding. I try to kneel again by the gushing, crystal water and, like an idiot, lose my footing. I grope for the bank for something to grab hold of but it is as if the river itself pulls me in and I am dragged to the deepest water, spluttering and fighting for breath. Invisible hands, strong as ten men, take me and draw me down into the dark underworld of the river. I am submerged, held fast like a fish in a net, floundering and gasping. The water is beyond cold. It fills me up. It is in my mouth, my ears, up my nose, everywhere. It numbs every part of me and I think my brain might freeze. Is this the sacrifice they want – my death by drowning? It doesn't seem so. That same unseen hand grips and propels me upwards, forces me out into the air like a babe from its mother's womb, and like a babe I emerge learning to breathe again, coughing and crying, reborn. The goddess of this water does not want me dead. Is it her hand which steers me on to the gentlest slopes of the bank some distance downstream? I don't know.

I make a graceless landing, but I manage to haul myself on to dry land without too much trouble. I am so cold my teeth chatter. I strip off my clothes including the mail shirt which should have drowned me had I not been in the river's care. I disrobe slowly; my hands are too cold to do otherwise and it is as if I am peeling off the skin of an onion, layer by layer, until all that is left is me, Trista. My skin feels as raw as if I have been pared down right to my core. I am gasping for breath and laughing hysterically. I am no longer trembling: my limbs are lean but strong again. I hold out my arm and it is steady as stone. My bruises have disappeared, my sliced palm is healed, my slave mark is gone. I am clean and cold, whole and free.

I can't quite believe it. I lay my clothes on the bank to dry, wring out my hair and dance around for a while in joy and celebration and more practically to get my blood flowing so I don't die of the cold. It is as if I have never been a slave. I am the woman I was before I was enslaved: strong and fit. When I am dry, I drop my mail shirt, Lucius' helmet and the Chief's sword into the fast-flowing current in gratitude. It is a suitable offering – more or less everything that I have. All I keep are those things that have been given to me. It is not seemly to give away gifts so I keep my clothes, my spear, my wolf ring, the druid's gift and the message for Caratacus. I have been washed clean by a sacred river and all I have to give should be given. In any case those things that are tainted with blood and acquired through other people's sacrifice properly belong to the gods; they do not belong to me. I say a brief prayer that is more or less incoherent, and watch my stolen tools of war sink into the sacred water. I am Trista, a warrior seeress, and I pay my debts.

CHAPTER TWENTY-FIVE

Trista's Story

As soon as the clothes are dry I start walking again – this time without need of my spear.

The druids' walk follows the path of this most holy of rivers for a time. I have to resist the urge to run along it. No one knows what a gift fitness is until they no longer have it. The Wild Weird join me in greater numbers as I leave the sacred grove behind me.

I feel as safe now as if I were playing in the coppiced woods of my childhood home. The gods of this place have blessed me; what do I have to fear? Even the Weird are subject to their command. The night is crisp and the sky so bright with unfamiliar stars, I wonder if I'm even in the same world I left only hours ago. I'm not hungry, though it is a long time since I ate the fireside meal with Ger and his horde. I'm not thirsty and I don't feel tired. Indeed I follow the shining road all through the night.

I've got used to the presence of the Weird, and am learning to ignore them as much as possible. They are not all small and though some resemble animals, most are like nothing I've ever seen before. They ignore me. Snake creatures slither over my feet, coil around my legs, flying things barely miss my head with their leathery wings, and some of the walking beings are so close I would feel their breath on my skin if they breathed. I walk for a while with two many-limbed creatures by my side. They are locked in an embrace that at times seems to include me and though I cannot feel their skin against mine, their closeness is still disturbing. I am used to living with visions of the dying. I can deal with this. I am unprepared for what happens next. One of these creatures pauses in the act of caressing its fellow to loosen, then remove my arm ring. It happens too swiftly, too unexpectedly, for me to prevent it. I don't see what happens next because suddenly the night is dark, cloudy and wet. I am shivering. The Wild Weird are gone and my feet are ankle-deep in cold mud. Worse, not five paces away two wolves turn at the sound of my horrified gasp.

I reach for my sword, but of course it's not there. Rain soaks through the wool of my tunic. I have no mail either to protect my heart. The nearest wolf moves towards me. My only remaining weapon is my gift of fire. I have to try to kindle my inner flame, without myself breathing fire. I don't want to endure the pain of that again. There are a couple of fallen branches nearby, rotten, wet and too big for me to lift. I find my inner heat and will the mound of wood into flame. The wolves are becoming bolder, moving together as if preparing to attack. The pile of wood resolutely refuses to ignite. There is movement behind me and a third wolf appears. If I can't light the wood, I will be at the mercy of this wild pack. I am breathing in a frightened panicky way and I know I need to be calm to find the fire in me. I need to be composed to fan the ember of my will and control the power so that it doesn't come pouring out of my mouth. My heart is hammering and all I can think about is being torn apart. They will be on me in a moment.

Something growls. I try not to listen. I don't want to see what is coming for me. I close my eyes and steady myself. Finally the wet wood catches and blazes, spitting and crackling as only wet wood can. I feed it my strength and it burns higher than a man, though the rain is coming down hard now and would have extinguished a lesser fire.

The wolves are backing away. I sprint to the shelter of the billowing flames and then I see him: the huge grey wolf, Morcant.

He snarls and his mouth is a cavern, the sound is a roar. There is no doubt that he is the strongest wolf there has ever been: the other wolves run. He is bigger even than the last time I saw him – twice the size of my potential attackers and his shadow self, my Morcant, is so clear, so real I think I might touch him. He is awake and watching me. I can't believe he is here. Did the Wild Weird expel me from the druids' walk on purpose?

The shadow man opens his arms as if to embrace me. I want to run to him, to tell him about my restoration, the return of my strength, everything that has happened. I dart forward. I am almost close enough to touch him. It would be a comfort just to stroke his wolf's pelt, to be certain that he is real and not some phantom. And then I see her, the she-wolf standing guard over her mate. She waits a pace or two behind him. She bares her teeth and a low growl, harsh and menacing, issues from her throat. I don't need any special insight to know what that means. This is real. I hesitate mid-stride, held captive by my uncertainty, frozen. I don't know if Morcant the wolf will protect me. His yellow wolf's eyes meet mine. Is there regret in them? The man raises a ghostly hand as if to touch me and then lets it fall. He bows his head as if in defeat. Why does he not become a man? Why doesn't he come back to me? I take a step back. The man raises his head and smiles, a smile that would break any heart let alone one as brittle as mine. I think I may have lost him.

My fire still blazes. I move to stand in the intense heat of its flames. I am certain the blaze will keep the she-wolf away.

She places herself next to the wolf and nuzzles against him. Her message is clear and Morcant does nothing to discourage her. I hope that he might give me some sign that I am as welcome by his side as she is: he does not.

Instead he stares at me steadily with unblinking yellow eyes. They do not lack intelligence, only warmth. This wolf has made his choice.

There is nothing to say. I am not diminished. I am Trista still. I can light fires and prophesy and fight as well as any man. If I must manage without Morcant, I can and will. I find myself twisting the wolf ring. In my imagination Gwyn is laughing. He would be amused to find me bested by a she-wolf.

The rain is soaking through my clothes and I start to shiver, the ordinary kind of shivering that afflicts everyone. My face is wet with the relentless rain and not with the tears that I will not let myself shed. What if the fireside tales are true and a week spent in the summer country could be a year or more in ours? How long has Morcant been the wolf?

CHAPTER TWENTY-SIX

Morcant's Story

The grey people have done their work after all. I give them thanks for they at least can hear me. She left no sound, no scent to follow, nothing. It was as if she'd been swallowed up by the earth. I'd never have found her without them.

She is surrounded by a gathering of the strange creatures; more join her every moment. The wolf in me is disturbed, they smell so wrong: I am enchanted. I never knew such shadow things existed until I became a shadow myself.

The perfume of the penumbral kingdom clings to Trista honey-sweet and lemon-sharp in this country without lemons. It almost masks the musk and spiciness that is her own unique scent. She looks different too, straighter and less scrawny, no longer weary but strong and lithe. Her hair is longer and curls around her face, bright as the flames she conjures, and I long for fingers to tuck it out of her way.

I want to run to her, but I can't. I am as bound by duty as

a wolf as I was as a legionary. My she-wolf needs me and she has no one but me. She is an outcast thanks to me and likely to remain so. She bears the taint of my unnatural scent wherever she goes. She carries our pups. What kind of creature, man or beast, abandons a female in such condition? I watch Trista go, wishing I could explain. The wolf can only twitch his ears and drop his tail and that she cannot understand.

Why doesn't her presence make me change? Finding her again should transform me as it has before yet my paws remain inflexible, clawed, fur-covered, not hands. My mouth is still an animal's maw, good for biting and tearing and shredding, useless for talking. Useless for kissing. Oh, Trista! I was so busy cursing my condition I forgot to be grateful for ever being a man at all. May the gods of this place forgive me if I offended them.

I follow her, keeping a safe distance between us. The camped men have dogs and I have no desire to kill them if they are set on me. She's lost her armour and her weapons and I don't like to see her enter the place of many men without either. There is danger there. There is blood in the air and the promise of more.

The rain brings out the stench of the not long buried dead and the bitter tang of war is on my tongue. I don't need her gift of prophecy to know what is to come.

The armies are amassing. The men of steel will fight the men of bone and all of the shadow world holds its breath, waiting to know the outcome. I'll gladly fight with the bone men, the tribespeople, with Trista, but I doubt they'll let me close enough to fight.

My poor she-wolf is weary and fearful. I've dragged her where she doesn't belong to follow Trista whom she doesn't trust. I must find her a place to rest now that dawn is nearly here. She is worthy of something better than a half-wolf, but the only wolf she wants is me.

CHAPTER TWENTY-SEVEN

Trista's Story

I try to remember where I was standing when the ring was lost and then I drop to my knees on the sodden ground and struggle to discover it by touch alone. Perhaps the Wild Weird kept it for themselves. I've almost given up all hope of finding it when my fingers close over something hard buried in the mud and stinking muck. As soon as I touch it, the grey folk appear all around me and the druids' walk glows like a beacon in the darkness, barely a pace away. I dry the ring on my cloak. It gleams as if lit by the warm sun of the summer country. I could use it to light my way through the night. I replace it reverently on my arm and get ready to step back on to the safety of the druids' road. Something makes me hesitate and it is not that I mistrust easy ways. What if the Wild Weird who guided me on to it had a reason for forcing me to leave it? Nobody knows how the Wild Weird think, least of all me. The druid of my childhood home did not prepare me for such experiences so I can only follow my instincts and they are screaming that this is not the way for me.

The path still tempts me but I turn my back on it and resign myself to the cold, wet, night of my homeland. There is some kind of settlement nearby.

I am thoroughly drenched. Rain trickles down the back of my neck. It would be good to discover that the savoury smell of woodsmoke and cooking belong to my own people, but I have too many enemies now to be anything other than extremely cautious. The source of the smoke lies beyond a steep ridge, hidden from view.

I need to become invisible, like the wolf, to investigate further. My arms are already caked in mud, so I plaster my face with it and hide my hair under my shawl. It has grown noticeably so that it touches my shoulders. Does that mean I've been away from this world for months? I drop into a kind of crouching run, hiding behind trees when I can, trying to get closer to the ridge without being seen. The presence of the grey folk is distracting – their movements constantly catch my eye. I need to be alert for real dangers. Regretfully I remove Ger's armband and put it into my belt pouch. The landscape is barren without the Weird. I've grown accustomed to their ghostly companionship. I miss my sword more, however. Whoever is camped here will have set a watch and sent scouts and I don't even have a belt knife to protect me.

Someone is following me, I'm sure. I sense rather than hear the sound. I turn and come face to face with the wolf.

He has become better at being the wolf since we last met. He makes no sound at all. I on the other hand have to suppress a scream of shock. 'Morcant!' I want to shout out my delight but suppress that too so that all that escapes my lips is a half-swallowed whisper. I bury my muddy face in the soft fur of his back.

He allows me to embrace him for a time. But I haven't entirely lost my wits and I pull myself together quickly.

I look into the eyes of the wolf. 'Morcant, do you know who is camped over there? Are they Kelts or Romans?'

The wolf makes a sound at the back of his throat, a soft sound between a growl and a whine, modulated like speech. It is as if the beast is trying to speak and his effort brings tears to my eyes. I can't understand him however I strain, and the wolf drops his tail and ears with disappointment. I stroke his head.

'Never mind. It was worth a try.' It is only then that I notice Morcant the shadow man's frantic efforts to attract my eye. He is miming a salute. We have no such greeting and his meaning is clear. 'They are Roman?'

The wolf does not nod, but somehow he gives his assent. My heart sinks. I thought things were going too well. Somehow I've run into the legions again. Does that mean I am still far from Caratacus or that I am close and a battle is imminent? I wriggle forward, up to the top of the ridge. The mud is icy and slippery, squelching under my knees and making it difficult to gain any purchase on the bank. I have to grab on to Morcant's fur a couple of times to prevent myself falling back down the way I've come. When I get to the top, I flatten myself against the ground and peer at the biggest gathering of people I have ever seen.

The encampment stretches as far as I can see. Tents arranged in rows, so many straight lines, following the pattern of the fortress of the Ninth. Cook fires are brilliant splashes of orange in the grey dawn and wind-blown rain, which throws a billowing cloak of silver-grey across the scene. There is a great deal of mud and most of that is grey too, as if some enchantment has leached the world of colour.

I am not very good at reckoning but I count the rows and the number of tents per row. Someone with greater gifts than I might be able to calculate the force that musters here. For now it is time to withdraw and find the army I wish to join.

I explain what I need to do to the wolf. I know that Morcant understands for the silver shadow, rendered grey as the rest of the world by the ceaseless rain, scowls. When I look back, he has gone.

The other wolves dropped a half-eaten carcass of a hare in an effort to escape Morcant. I do what I can with my bare hands to scrape out the innards and skewer the meat with a sharp stick to cook it over the flames.

When I have eaten my fill of meat that is either burned or raw, I follow the sound of running water. The sun has finally returned some muted colour to the grey world, though the rain has not ceased. The source of the sound is not far away – a small waterfall and a fast-flowing river of clear water. I give thanks to the goddess. All water for me is precious now for it may be some tributary of the sacred water that restored me. I wash the grease from my hands and drink deeply. My eye is caught by the flash of something bright in among the dark rocks that constrict the river's flow and make it gush downwards in a great torrent. It is not the best time to be curious. I can't allow myself to forget how close I am to a vast army of enemies, but I am waiting for Morcant and anything that distracts me from the possibility that he may not return is a blessing.

I am so wet already, I think nothing of wading into the freezing water, trusting to the goddess's good grace. If she wished to drown me, she would not have saved me. The cold water makes me gasp and washes away my camouflage. I am wide awake and shivering convulsively.

Something is definitely wedged in the sharp rocks, something that catches the pale sunlight and flashes silver. I am glad of my newly restored strength because the only way to reach the elusive object is to climb up the rocks and stretch my arm to its fullest extent. I am quickly drenched by water so cold it takes my breath away, but my blue hands touch smooth steel. I gasp as the water flows all round and over me then stretch still more. My fingers close on something and I pull. It resists and I pull harder and finally I have it in my hand. It has lost all its gems and the carved hilt is much the worse for wear but its perfect weight and glorious balance mark it as my stolen sword returned to me! I offered it to the goddess and she refused the gift, taking only that which marked it as precious to those who are not warriors. Its true beauty lies in its flexibility, its razor edge and the perfection of its length and weight and movement. The goddess has granted me a great boon. I don't have to think for long. I twist the wolf's head ring from my finger. It was mine before I gave it to Gwyn, lost then restored to me. It is mine to give. I have no need of a wolf charm when I have a wolf beside me. Gwyn is dead. I have in my own way grieved for him. He would have traded that ring for a sword any day so I am without guilt; he would have traded me for a sword if it came to that. Goodbye, Gwyn. May you be granted a happy rest or a grand rebirth. As I watch the ring sink below the spindrift of the white water I feel free of his shade at last.

I light a fire and strip off because even I am not stupid

enough to risk an ague. I use my belt as a strop to hone the edge of my restored blade, while my clothes dry and I warm myself in the heat of my fire. I don't know why the gods have chosen to bless me but I'm grateful. My only worry is that they may want a greater sacrifice from me at the end.

I dress again as if for battle. My hair isn't yet long enough to plait and I have nothing with which to tie it back. It hangs around my face getting in my way. I may have to hack it short again. I check my precious possessions. Against all odds, I still have the scratched bark message and Ger's arm ring. I also have the wolf. When I turn from the fire, he is standing there watching me. I didn't even hear him return.

I put out my fire. I took a great risk in lighting it. The wolf nuzzles my hip where I've hung the sword from my pouch. Morcant the silver ghost raises his eyebrow in question. 'It was a gift of the goddess,' I say. May the remainder of our journey be as blessed. I put my hand on the thick ruff of fur around the wolf's great neck. His head is level with the crook of my elbow and we walk easily together. The man touches my arm and it is like walking with the Wild Weird. Thus entwined I let the beast lead me round the Roman encampment.

We have to travel some distance cross-country, looping around the camp. I depend on the wolf's superior senses when he bolts for cover and do my best to follow him. He is so quick. I have a couple of grazes from where I flung myself into a ditch. At least this landscape provides plenty of cover.

Some time before noon we hide for what seems like a whole watch when we come across a Roman chief and his retinue. They are so noisy we were in no danger of being surprised by them, but for some reason Morcant chooses to stay close to them and wait for them to pass. The men are all on horseback and are extravagantly decked out in polished armour. I worry that the horses' terrified response to Morcant's scent might cause the men to dismount and investigate, but while the horses buck, their riders battle for control and, regaining it, urge them on. Trained by my father to trust my mount, I find this surprising. A couple of the less important men carry standards and a golden eagle. Perhaps this is another of their gods and they are too confident in its protection to worry about roadside ambushes or prowling beasts.

Most of the men ride without speaking but the one I assume is a chief shouts to another over the sounds of their progress: jangling harnesses, clanking armour and pounding hoofbeats. The wolf cocks his head as if listening hard. Morcant can understand their jabbering – if only he could translate if for me. We don't move until even the wolf can no longer hear their clamour. The wolf looks pleased with himself and I gather that the men said something useful. He sniffs the air and leads me on, loping ahead with even greater speed and confidence so that I have to run to keep up. Only when I'm breathless and clutching my side does he take pity on me and slow his pace. I've no wind even to complain.

By late afternoon we come to a broad river. I didn't know that a wolf could look smug, but he does and I guess from this unexpected expression that this is the River Sabrina, which marks the boundary with the western tribes, the Silures. I know few people who have travelled so far. As far as I know, my own tribe has no quarrel with them, but our trade and exchange with such a far-flung group has been limited. I am nervous. The wolf and I must be a strange sight, walking together. I know that we are watched. The hills ahead are full of eyes and the land to our backs is not without observers. The back of my neck prickles. I get a flash of prophecy – the river is clogged with bodies, the muddy waters streaked with red. I tighten my grip on the wolf's ruff of coarse hair. Morcant the ghost gives me a wan smile. This river is a serious obstacle to the invaders and crossing it will be no easy thing. I think of the vast army of legionaries we've left behind. How will so many men cross this? Caratacus has chosen his base well. It is not just an obstacle to our enemies, it is an obstacle for me. With the goddess's blessing I might try to swim it, but I don't know how the wolf would feel about that. In any case I have no proper scabbard for my sword and I will not lose it again.

The land here is flat and waterlogged, becoming marsh of the kind to drown the unwary and those unfamiliar with the territory. I hesitate. Why has the wolf chosen this crossing place? It seems to me to be a death trap. Once we leave the firm ground we could be stuck up to our middles in mud, picked off like sitting ducks by spears from either side.

I still rest my hand on his thick fur. It is a comfort to be close to him and it is with an effort of will that I let him go so that he can take the lead. He lifts his head and sniffs the air and as I turn back I see them: the mounted men I thought we'd lost, riding across the plain towards us. They ride on sandy ground, mirrored by standing water. Each stride sends an arc of bright spray flying into the air. It seems we have no choice now. I have no desire to fight mounted men. I pick up my tunic, hitch it over my belt and start to wade. There is no time to be over-cautious. I have to trust to the Lady of Sabrina, the goddess of this water, to see us over to the other side. I dare not look back, but now I can hear the rumble of hoofs on the soft ground, the jangle of metal and the heavy breathing of the horses. They may find this terrain even more difficult than I do as the weight of man and horse will sink them deep into the mire. Not that the bog will necessarily be a problem for them. They don't have to follow me; all they have to do is stop me and a spear flung from the horse's back will do that very well.

The wolf is some distance ahead of me, finding firm ground with an unerring instinct. I wonder how he does it until I see the shadow of Morcant gesturing to me desperately. The sunlight makes it harder to see his silvery spectre. He is miming something. The ring? The ring! I struggle a little with my belt pouch and my sword. I am terrified of dropping either of these most precious objects into the mud. I fumble clumsily, almost dropping it. My muscles tremble with the after-effects of my flight and with fear too, but it's all right. I slip Ger's arm ring up over my wrist and push it as far up my arm as I can. Suddenly I see what Morcant wishes me to: the grey folk guiding our steps, leading the way. I try to run, though my tunic is a hindrance, and once more four legs prove themselves more stable than two. There are two grey creatures in front of me – a fox-headed homunculus and something else that defies description – they are pointing awkwardly with deformed limbs towards firmer ground. That is all very well, but I am caught and the horsemen are coming nearer. I duck down, trying to hide under the reeds and scrubby vegetation, but there is nothing else to see on this flat flood plain but me, the wolf and a few seabirds. The wolf is surprisingly difficult to spot, blending into the sandy mud so that his darker markings look like clumped reeds or shadow. I know that my hair in sunshine is bright enough to be a spearman's target in this place of muted greys and sandy browns. I try to hide it with my shawl.

I have my sword raised and ready. That is all that I can do. The pounding hoofs are nearer and the men shout to one another. I squat down in the mud so that it reaches up to my shoulders. I keep the sword up and out of the mud so that it looks for all the world like a needle emerging from sackcloth. I stay very still and try to ignore the efforts of the Wild Weird, who are intent on showing me the firm pathway to Morcant, never mind that it is no use to me at this moment, when all that matters is that the horsemen cannot see me well enough to splice me with their spears. They are very near now. A bird hurls itself into the sky so close to me that I'm startled. It is desperately trying to take off in advance of the charging men. I duck, and in the motion my shawl slips from my hair and I know I am seen. A spear flies – a good shot; it lands barely a hand's breadth away. I am about to get to my feet. I may get a chance at one of them at least, but then I hear the growl of the wolf and the startled shouts of the mounted men. The wolf has abandoned all attempts at camouflage and is running straight for them. He is sure-footed and fast. The horses rear. One man falls and is hauled upright by his desperate comrades who seem to have forgotten their spears and their swords in favour of flight.

I don't waste the distraction; I know he risked himself for me. I pull the spear from the bog with no little difficulty and then use it as a staff to help me stay on my feet as I wade as quickly as I can towards the firmer ground. I move with such haste that I don't test the depth of the mud with the spear's end but simply follow the urging of the grey folk. They are dancing around with great agitation and I take that as a sign that I should hurry.

There is a pathway of sorts, reinforced by stones but so well hidden that anyone unaware of its whereabouts could spend days looking for it. I glance over my shoulder. The wolf has done his job. I am sure the mounted men were unnerved by the sight of a monstrous beast appearing from nowhere in the middle of the day and were startled into flight. I am certain they will regroup and return. We don't have much time to make our escape. I begin to run or rather squelch along this stone road before the cavalry regroup and return. Morcant is back beside me in twenty long paces and in his mouth he carries a cavalry shield. He drops it at my feet like a hunting dog presenting his kill.

'Thanks,' I say, because without him I would have stood little chance. The shield is a cause for gratitude too. It is a little damp and chewed at its leather edges now, but a good thing to have. I sling it over my back by its long, leather strap and keep moving along the narrow causeway. Much to my surprise the causeway continues over the broad river itself. I don't know what I would do without the grey folk leading me and the wolf following behind so that I can't turn back. The stones must be pillars sunk into the river's bed, invisible to the eye, lying just below the surface of the water. Each step is a leap of faith, for it looks as if I will plunge into the depths of this great river. Each time my feet find the safety of a flat rock, I sing my tuneless little song of thanks to the goddess, though I don't think the wolf is impressed by my musicality. I don't know what the grey folk think, if indeed they think anything at all.

CHAPTER TWENTY-EIGHT

Trista's Story

We are met at the other side by a deputation of two men, heavily armed, and an escort of some twenty spear-wielding warriors. I think the latter are for the wolf's benefit because I'm sure one muddy girl would not justify such a show of force. I quietly remove the arm ring and slip it back into its pouch. I can't afford to be distracted here.

There is nothing I can do to look less disreputable. I resist the urge to smooth my hair. I don't know if Morcant senses my discomfort but the wolf stands very close beside me and seems happy for me to rest my hand once more on his back. I have tied the sword to my belt and wrapped it in my cloak so that it does not cut me. I carry the spear in my right hand, the shield over my shoulder. Whatever I look like I have no doubt that it is not a warrior.

There is a distinct air of unease as I approach the waiting men. They glitter with gold; their thick torques glint in the steely light. Precious stones stud their belts, their fingers, their scabbards, and blue tribal tattoos wind, like ivy, up their arms. Their trews and cloaks are of fine wool, woven into complex patterns and bright as if newly dyed.

'Who showed you our route across the river?' It is the taller of the two men who speaks. His accent is unfamiliar, difficult to understand. There are no preliminaries, no introductions, but at least his sword remains sheathed. These people don't know if we are friends or enemies. When I remember the vast encampment full of our steel-armoured invaders, I sympathise. However, it does not do to be too meek and humble with men such as these – that at least I know.

'I am Trista, a warrior of the Brigante and a seeress; this is Morcant, a shapeshifter. We were guided across the water by the Wild Weird. We have travelled here because we have a message for Caratacus.' I speak slowly and clearly, reasoning that the problem of understanding might run in both directions, but I make sure that I show the bravado fitting for a bloodied warrior of a bloody tribe.

There is no response for a moment. I wait. Surely these people are not just another variety of foe? Is it possible that I've made a mistake in coming here?

The wind buffets the cloaks of the assembled warriors as if they are sails. It ruffles Morcant's thick coat. It catches my hair and whips it into my mouth, bringing with it the taste of salt and the scent of fish. Above, seagulls circle, cawing noisily. Here on the river bank no one moves a muscle. No one makes a sound. The silence stretches and I wonder if there was some password I was supposed to know, something else I should have said to have them know me as an ally. I am about to break with all usual etiquette and speak again, but finally the man replies.

'I saw your little game of cat and mouse with the cavalry over there – was that staged for our benefit?' His tone is much clearer than his heavily accented words. He is still hostile.

I am gripping my spear so tightly that my knuckles are white. The wolf is as restless as I am and I suspect that he too is deciding who to attack if things do not go as we expect. The wind tries to steal the words away before I've even got them out. I have to shout to be heard. I bellow like I'm calling children in from the fields. It isn't very dignified. 'No, of course not! I am a tribeswoman and my companion a shapeshifter and both of us have come to lay our talents at the service of a leader worthy of the loyalty of the tribes.'

The second man nods. I can't hear what he says because he puts his mouth hard against his companion's ear, but the next moment he gives a hand signal and the spearman surge forward to surround us. The wolf growls.

'Our men will escort you to Caratacus,' the tall man says in response. I notice that his hand hovers nervously near his sword and that he does not take his eyes off Morcant.

'I trust that you will give us a safe passage,' I say as coolly as my dry mouth allows. 'The wolf is quick to anger and I'm not slow.'

The spearmen surround us all right, but are careful to keep a healthy distance between the wolf and their own vulnerable hides.

We are marched away from the broad river and along a narrow gully towards the hills beyond. At every stage we are challenged by tribesmen who stare at me and at Morcant as if we are creatures from the other world, which might just about be fair in Morcant's case but is hardly so in mine. I am beginning to get irritated by their endless scrutiny and it is only the spectral hand of Morcant the man on my flesh and blood arm that keeps me calm.

By the time we reach the peak of the nearest hill the sun has come out and the grey world has turned blue. I have to squint to see the several large timber buildings that have been constructed in something approaching the Roman style. There is also an open-sided building much like the stalls at the vicus outside Morcant's fort. It is furnished with all the opulence of a King's hall and is occupied by several people in the rich clothes of the tribal nobility. I am dazzled by the display of wealth. The tall warrior who escorted me here addresses one of them with a bow.

'Lord, we have brought them,' he says. I think I see someone who looks a bit like Ger seated by the campfire, but it can't be him. I left him far away just a day ago. I squint against the now bright sun to get a better look, but then a man stands up, separates himself from the bright melee and walks towards me. All other thoughts fly from my head. He is not naked and in chains, as I have so often seen him in my dreams, he is flamboyantly dressed in tribesman fashion, but it is still unmistakably him. His handsome face is smiling. I've never seen him smile. I am afraid that I might collapse with shock. My life has finally caught up with my visions. The man who has haunted them since I was a child stands before me. Does that mean my life is about to end?

He is younger than I thought him, but then when I first dreamed of him I was a little girl and all men seemed old to me then. I sway a little and it is lucky that I can lean on the wolf. The man of my dreams is courteous and courageous. He sees my difficulty and comes to assist me. Bowing to the wolf, he guides me to a fur-covered couch. He pours cool water into a silver goblet and hands it to me. I avoid making contact with his elegant hands. I am confused. Am I a prisoner or not?

In my mind's eye I get a flash of those other times I've seen

211

him – naked and in chains walking through a city made of stone, a Roman city I am sure, perhaps even Rome itself.

I've seen him stripped, whipped and humiliated, weeping, gritting his teeth against pain, but I've never seen him like this.

'Lady, are you well?' His voice is soft and though his accent is not mine, I have no trouble in understanding him. His face is as familiar to me as my lost brothers' and it is strange that he doesn't know me at all. I try to smile, but I fear that the effect is less than friendly.

'I am well, thank you. I did not expect to see you here, that's all.'

He frowns, 'Forgive me if we have met before, but the occasion escapes me.' I shake my head.

'I am sorry. It's hard to explain.' I take a sip from the goblet.

Although the man is friendly, our escort still waits, surrounding the wolf. All around us are armed warriors alert and ready for violence. I steady myself and try to behave with the gravitas of a visionary.

'I am a warrior and seeress of the Brigante. I have seen you in my visions since I was a child.'

He looks at me curiously. I feel stupid. He is so finely dressed that he is obviously a man of great importance and I ought to know who he is. It takes a moment and then the realisation comes. This, the man of my dreams, is the man everyone has been talking about: Caratacus of the Catuvellauni, the leader of the Keltic rebels. He looks like a leader. His blue eyes are very piercing. He is undoubtedly the best-looking tribesman I've ever seen. I remember my childhood belief that he was to be my husband and become hotter and more uncomfortable still. He pats my arm in a gesture somewhere between a comradely embrace and avuncular reassurance. I see him bloodied, naked and in chains, and the vision image is as real as the flesh and blood image before me. I sway and might have fallen were I not already safely seated.

'I have a message, sir, from a lady. She asked me to give you this.'

I grapple inelegantly for the pouch at my waist, conscious of the many eyes upon me and of the silver shadow of Morcant staring at me with a most disgruntled expression.

'Ah. You are also a rebel fighter then?' I wonder if he is laughing at me. I'm sure I've never looked less like a fighter.

'I am a warrior, sir,' I say with pride of my own. 'I fight whoever tries to hurt me and mine.' I sit up straighter and feel a fool.

He reaches over and touches my hand. 'My dear, I was not taunting you. I see by your hands that you are used to the sword at your waist and your fierce eyes mark you as a fighter. I am anxious only that your commitment to our cause be properly recognised.' The armed men around me do not stand down and I am not reassured.

He takes some time to study the now damp bark on which Cassie scratched the marks of which she was so proud. When he speaks, it is to the other men and women assembled round him.

'The Queen's consort, Venutius, may have been too optimistic. If this missive is true, it seems that Cartimandua, our Queen of the Brigante, is still paying her Roman dues. If she is to join us, I don't think it will be yet.' He sighs. 'She is a wily politician as likely to do one thing and say another as any man I've met but we will have to proceed without her, for now at least.'

There is much murmuring at that, but I can't catch any of the words. It seems clear to me that this news is a blow to him and perhaps to the others assembled there. I seem to have stumbled upon a council of war. I never thought that this message, that was so precious to Cassie, would matter at all to anyone else. I only delivered it out of duty. I revise my estimation of Cassie yet again. It seems that she is not only a spy but a useful one.

He turns his attention towards me again. 'We are grateful to you for carrying this news, however unwelcome to us. Ger had prepared us for the arrival of a great seer, but I see you are more than that.'

I look towards the fireside. It is Ger! He greets me with a shy, gap-toothed smile.

'There is a great army gathering against us. If we can defeat it before it reaches our holiest lands, then we may yet preserve our heritage. You at least have arrived in time for the fun.' He sounds grim and the effect of his words is not much softened by his smile. I know little of tribal politics, but even I understand that my Queen commands numberless warriors and, with her support, Caratacus could expect an army of ferocious, well-trained Brigante fighters to swell his ranks. I know that he doesn't think he can win the battle that is certainly coming without them, or rather us, for I should by rights be part of that Brigante army. I fear that he cannot win it either, for what victor travels to the stronghold of his enemies in chains?

'Sir, there is more.' Finally he waves my armed escort away and I tell him of the encampment I have seen. He sends slaves to bring a tray of flat damp sand and a narrow golden dagger which I use to mark the layout of the camp. I smooth it away and try to shape the sand into the form of the landscape around the camp.

Ger looks grave. 'Our seeress here estimates the numbers of legionaries at around twenty thousand – which fits with our other intelligence.'

'We'd better get a move on with the fortifications then.' I don't know who speaks but it is a woman's voice and after that I lose track. Perhaps it is exhaustion, perhaps it is the

215

gods' revenge for my days of freedom from my visions, but suddenly I am beset by them: Caratacus in chains again, Morcant the man, a white corpse, the Parisi pedlar burning and screaming, Ger's druid on fire, and everywhere in every vision now the grey folk are there, watching.

CHAPTER TWENTY-NINE

Morcant's Story

I can't stay here where there is the stench of men, their cooking, their fires, their middens and their graves. Where there are so many tribesmen there are accidents and several fights have yielded mortal wounds. Man-stink buries all other scents. It makes me angry and I know I walk with hackles raised. I am protected by the word of Caratacus, but wherever I go by I see murder in men's eyes. Others come to stare at me as if I am a wonder. There are many warriors whose throats look ripe for the ripping and it is hard not to snarl and worse.

Trista is gone, cared for by Caratacus' women, kept close because of her gifts. She is lost, laid low by visions, and even the sweet-smelling grey ones can't reach her. There are druids here. I've heard they are sending for more – more soothsayers and philosophers, diviners and tale-tellers. I listen to the talk of this camp but little of it makes any sense.

One thing is certain, I don't want to see any druids; I keep out of their way. There is talk that there are other shapeshifters too, but in all the confusion of man-stink I've not detected their scent. I am a wolf now. I was a soldier. I was a shapeshifter. Now I am a simply a wolf.

I will fight when the time comes because Trista will fight and she will have need of my teeth, my claws, my strength and my ferocious power. Now I must answer the needs of the wolf. My mate has come for me, crossed the wide river at a narrower point and found me. She howls for me and I must go. I have told the grey folk to try to tell Trista I will return. Trista will understand, but I don't think the grey folk do.

CHAPTER THIRTY

Trista's Story

In the women's hall, where I'm tended by slaves and guarded by armed men, the visions are relentless. Mostly they are of places I've never seen and people I've never met, but that doesn't make their deaths any less terrible. One of the slaves helps lift me into a seating position and props me up on skins and pillows. A young woman is there to meet me.

'Trista?'

She is young, barely older than me, and she is carrying a baby.

'They say you know what is to come?'

I nod. 'Sometimes.'

'Tell me. Do we survive?'

Oh no. Not this. I dread this question above all else. 'We all die, lady,' I say. 'In the end none of us survive.' I know she is going to make me touch her or the child or something and then I will see what neither of us wants me to see. Her gaze is steady, unblinking.

'I have three children. All I want to know is if it would be better for me to take them and hide somewhere or follow duty and stay with my husband.'

'Your husband?'

'Caratacus.'

I am shocked. I am more disturbed when I understand why. In some secret part of myself I still thought that Caratacus and I might be destined for each other. Why else would he dominate my dreams? I hide my confusion by requesting a drink. The slaves give me wine, though I would have preferred water.

'I can't advise you – my gift is too erratic . . .'

'Please.'

She reaches out her hand, which is plump and white and has never toiled in the fields or wielded a sword. I take it. As ever, I am somewhere else in an instant and I have to pull my hand away, panting for breath.

'What is it? What happens to my children?' She looks alarmed and I realise that it has taken courage to come to me, to face what has to be faced.

'I did not see this battle . . .' She clutches her baby to her as if the very word fills her with fear. 'I see you playing with two children, your children, somewhere else. I don't know where it is but you are in a fine room with servants all around, so you are safe.' She gives a strangled cry between a sigh and a sob. Because I am a seeress I am compelled to add, 'The baby is not with you there. I see him in the arms of a running slave . . .'

'What happens to him?' She holds him so tightly I'm surprised he can breathe.

'I don't know. I'm sorry.' I fall back down on to the pillows, overcome by the familiar nausea and have to close my eyes.

When I next open them, some dreadful dreams later, she is gone.

After the visit by Caratacus' wife I receive a steady stream of supplicants and interrogators: a man in druid's robes, a warrior, or sometimes an old woman with her long white hair unbound and flowing over her shoulders. Once I am visited by a wolf. It is not Morcant and I think I may have dreamed him. It is hard to tell and I don't know what any of them want from me.

Caratacus comes as night approaches. My pallet is screened by thick and expertly woven hangings. It is quite private but for the guards and the slaves and he sends both away. This space is lit by Roman oil lamps for, though Caratacus dresses as a tribesman, he is fond of the invaders' innovations. I have heard that his home is a villa furnished and built in the Roman style with a bathhouse and even a temple where he worships the Roman gods alongside our own. These stories have reached me in the chatter of the

221

slaves and the guardsmen and I don't doubt them. Caratacus is not a simple man.

'Have you seen my future, Trista?' He whispers because it would not be good for us to be overheard. 'Are we victorious?' I am a seeress and I speak the truth. 'Sir, I don't think it ends in victory, or at least not for you.'

It is hard to say this to the vital, driven man in front of me. I want to make him happy and I can't – not if I'm true to all I believe about my gift. The expression that flits across his face is hard to read.

'I've been fighting the Roman invaders since they decided to make my lands theirs. I've been fighting to keep Alba in the hands of the tribes since before you were born. If the tribes united, we could end it now. If Cartimandua brought your countrymen south, we could trap the bulk of the enemy forces and finish them. They are not gods, you know, these Romans. They lack a good leader here. With the Brigante fighting with us, as well as the Silures and Ordovices, I couldn't fail. I can't fail.'

I daren't speak. Perhaps I am wrong, perhaps he wins, but I don't believe it.

'Have you seen this battle?' I shake my head. 'Then we can win?'

I can't lie. 'I don't know. Maybe you win this battle and lose the next?'

There is a pause – a long one. Caratacus doesn't want to believe me and perhaps it would be better for everyone if he did not. No one wants to go to war believing they are doomed. If anyone can make this work, it is Caratacus. I've only just met him and yet I know this.

'Have any of your visions yet failed to come to pass?'

'There are things I've seen that have not yet happened. Who is to say if they will come to pass or not? My gifts are strange, unreliable, but it may be that the gods brought me to you for a reason – so that you could make preparation . . .' I have a sudden memory of the destruction of the Chief's hall and fall silent. I think something of that remembrance might show on my face because he leans forward and squeezes me on my shoulder.

'I see that you are honest. Ger has already vouched as much. I will plan for success and prepare for failure. If we do not win, then all must withdraw to their homes. There will be no Keltic slaves from this venture. We must survive to fight another day.'

I know that he is talking as much to himself as to me. I sit up.

'I will fight for you,' I say, 'With Ger's men if he will have me.'

Caratacus nods. I can see that his mind is already on other arrangements. I think he has forgotten me, then he turns and gives me the full force of his smile. 'I will send you a scabbard,' he says and then is gone. I am surprised he noticed my lack.

I sleep then and at dawn slaves help me wash and ready myself. I ask them not to touch me with their hands because I don't wish to foresee their deaths. They accept that calmly as if they dealt with a seeress every day. They plait my hair in tiny plaits as they do in the furthest parts of Rome's Empire. I don't know how they know this, as they are both of them from the southern tribes of Alba, but it is a good way of keeping it out of my eyes. I note their slave brands and wince. I am careful to leave food on my plate in case they're hungry, but Caratacus treats his slaves better than my old Chief and they give the scraps to the dogs. One of them brings me new clothes, good boots and warm foot bindings, and a sword with a scabbard of worked gold that astounds me. They have a new sword belt for me too, that is decorated with gold and enamel. I have to rescue my own belt with its pouch before the slave can sweep it away. I keep the pouch with Ger's armband still inside it. I can't accept the gift of the sword. The Chief's sword was returned to me by the goddess of the water and only a fool would reject such a present. I explain that to the youngest of the slaves.

'I cannot give this sword to you, but you could perhaps keep it somewhere so that if all goes wrong you are not left weaponless.'

The look she gives me is forthright. I don't doubt that she has fought herself. Her hands are scored with a lattice of white scars of the kind we all get in training. 'Thank you, but you should keep it as a spare blade. If all goes as wrong as you suggest, there will be plenty of corpses to plunder and no one will go weaponless.' She is right, of course, on both counts. I have seen the heaped corpses of our tribal dead in my visions, but I did not lie to Caratacus. I don't know if they die now or at some other time. And it is true that everyone must die sometime.

Before I go in search of Ger I put on his gift to me. My dress bears witness to my loyalties to the goddess, to the Brigante fighters and to Caratacus. I need nothing from Morcant; some loyalties require no outward sign.

Ger greets me as one warrior greets another – a form of respect that pleases me more than it should. I've earned this right – to be greeted as an equal, but it is rare enough to gladden my heart.

'You shouldn't have left us as you did, Trista. We thought you were lost.'

He is looking at me with such affection and concern I feel a little overwhelmed.

'How long is it since I left your camp?'

'What do you mean? We lost all trace of you for two months.' So it is true that time passes differently on the druids' walk.

'It did not seem so long to me. It's some time since anyone worried about me. I'm sorry. I didn't intend to alarm you.'

'Ah well, Bethan blamed herself for letting you go, but you are here now and you will do me honour if you will fight beside me in this glorious fight!'

'The honour will be all mine,' I say and have the pleasure of seeing his gnarled face light in a smile of delight and pride.

They have no women warriors in their small group and the untrained women will fight only as a last resort. Ger has begged Caratacus to let us fight in the vanguard, for the honour of our tribe, otherwise absent. It is important to all of us that our fellow tribesmen remember that our reputation for toughness, courage and ferocity is not forgotten just because our Queen has absented us from this fight. I know Ger is ashamed of Cartimandua's alliance with Rome and his main worry is not death but dishonour. The word is coming in from all the lookouts that the Romans have finally forded the river. They will be with us within the next watch.

'I have to go and find the wolf.'

'He's gone, Trista. He did not stay long. Are you sure he is truly a shapeshifter? There's been howling these last nights. You must have heard it?'

I shake my head. I've been lost in my visions and fear their return at any moment. I've heard nothing but the screams of the dying for nights on end.

'He *is* a shapeshifter. You met his human self – you remember? He was my slave when I came to trade for your sword?'

Ger, it seems, is one of the many people who do not notice slaves.

I don't believe Morcant would leave me to fight this battle alone. We are fast running out of time. The battle horn has been sounded. The Romans are upon us and we must hear Caratacus' battle plan.

CHAPTER THIRTY-ONE

Trista's Story

My heart starts to pound. The last time I fought a battle rather than a skirmish I lost everything and everyone. I may not be as old as Ger, but we have this in common: we have no illusions about what is to come. I see it all in the look he gives me: fear, anxiety, pride, battle lust. The same feelings surge through me in much the same order. All my life I've been trained to fight. Since I was a child I've drilled and practised to this one end and I can't let my comrades down. I must show courage, skill and the will to survive, but I must be ready to die. This time I know what I'm getting myself into. If anything, it makes it harder.

Ger pats me on the shoulder. We understand each other. I check everything – sword, scabbard, shield, spear. I will fight as I always have without armour, though I'll be the first to admit that Roman mail is a thing of beauty and considerable usefulness.

The non-combatants, including Bethan, run for the shelter of the newly reinforced fort. She kisses Ger and hugs me. I can barely stand to look her in the eye. I know she wants to ask me what is to come and I cannot tell her. I don't know – not for sure. I am careful to avoid touching her flesh to flesh because I don't want to know. The battle is now and I have to focus on living entirely in this moment, if I am not to die. I pray to the goddess, to Taranis and Lugh, to every being who might influence our fate, that they might give us victory or welcome us if it is our time to die.

Caratacus and his deputies, tribal leaders all, stand on the high stone outer parapet of the hilltop stronghold. The rest of us throng around him. Out of habit I scan the crowd for faces I recognise as if I've forgotten that all my clan and kin are dead. For one brief moment I think I see the Parisi pedlar but it must have been some other redhead.

We begin by chatting and boasting to our fellows; little by little we lapse into silence, just as a creeping twilight becomes a total all-encompassing darkness. It is suddenly so quiet we can hear birdsong.

Caratacus, has of course, been druid trained in the arts of poetry and rhetoric. We are expecting a great feat of oratory. His powerful voice carries easily even in the open air. We demand no less.

'This not the time for grand speeches. We all know

what we are fighting for: our liberty from foreign invasion, our freedom to rule our own lands as we have always done in our own way. No warriors are braver, no fighters more courageous, no company more valorous than you, my comrades in arms, and it is an honour to fight with you this day.

'We will hold them off at the steepest point, the place we call "the wall", and there we will defeat them. They are numerous and well trained, well protected and well equipped but they have not your hearts, your passion, your might. But do not forget: this is not our final stand. When we have killed and slaughtered and destroyed and there is nothing more we can do, remember: we must withdraw, melt back into this our land, return to our own places so that we live to fight again, so we can crush and destroy our enemies, utterly.' He pauses; we expect him to go on.

'I trust in our gods, in you and in your strong arms and fearless hearts. To war!'

It must be the shortest battle speech we have ever heard, but we need little encouragement. He is right: we already know why we are here, putting aside our clannish enmities to make this stand against the men of steel. We scream our war cries back at him, building ourselves into the warrior frenzy that we will need if we are to do this. It is no easy thing to fight a man and try to kill him. It is impossible when the blood is cold and only a little less impossible when the blood burns with the fire of fury, the fervour of killing.

We run down the steep slope of the hillside in our thousands. I am part of a pack of my own, savage and uncontrolled but with a single purpose. We are like a herd of stampeding cattle: we could not stop if we wanted to. I strain to see if among this horde of screaming, maddened warriors, a lone wolf makes his own wild way to join us. There is no sign of him. I remove Ger's arm ring so that I can better see what lies in the real realm of scything swords and sharpened spears. The grey folk cannot help me here. I am no longer entirely Trista. I have become part of this barbarous battle horde and I am glad to be here. My blood boils and my heart beats to the rhythm of violence, the dark tattoo of destruction. I have gone beyond fear. If I am to die, so be it. Everyone dies sometime.

From our higher vantage point we have a clear view of the sea of silver that marches towards us, as if the River Sabrina has altered its course and grown spikes. It is hard not to feel a twisting in the guts and so we shout the more, taunting, boasting, cursing. For all that they are clad in silver, it is they that have to march uphill to us, for we have the higher ground.

I find myself a space to work. It would be foolishness to get tied up in the crush of men forging forward to be in the frontline, not because I am afraid but because they have left themselves too little room to move. Ger screams an order at his own men to stand back and I am relieved that we are of one mind in this too.

I shout to Ger that I am taking the higher ground and shake my spear. I can't see far enough to hit an enemy target in the throng down below. He nods and we work our way up, past our brothers in arms. I lack the wolf's senses but even I am almost overpowered by the sour sweat of my comrades, the pungent odour of this wild army.

The ground is a little wet still and I find a good position on a rock. I don't want to slip. Ger has done the same.

'Can we not call some of them back? They're too close together.' I am so worked up it is hard to talk. My blood is singing with the music of battle madness. A bit of me wants to join the closely packed crowd of men, though my head tells me again it is a fool's tactic.

He bellows, 'Pull back! Give your swords room to swing!' A few of the older, wiser heads pass the message on and many of the men take a step back. I note that the other female warriors are like me, finding firm ground from which to launch an attack. I nod at one dark-haired Silurian with a sharp little face and all the ferocity of a mad dog. She bares her teeth back at me and I'm reminded of the wolf. Morcant, where are you?

The war horns sound and the screaming rises to an even higher pitch. The Romans have war horns of their own and they too are blasting out over the yells of men. The vanguard of the Roman army has arrived. A drum rolls like thunder and a volley of stones lands among the advancing troops. I can't see that it will do much damage. At a blast of rapid notes from their horns, the Romans raise their shields over their heads to protect them from further assault. Our men set up a rhythmic chant, banging on their shields and chanting, drunk on war. High above us on the hill's top a druid, painted with symbols and sacred images and decked out in ritual robes, starts to intone the song of sacrifice. It is an uncanny noise, neither prayer nor chant but something in between. Her voice soars above all the other sounds of war and resonates within our very bones. It resounds around the hillside like thunder and everyone is silenced by it. There is power in it, that's for sure. Only when the last note dies down do we start our own war cries and taunts again.

The Romans struggle to gain any purchase on the slippery lower slopes of our natural citadel, but that doesn't help us much as our missiles bounce off their roof of shields. It is then that the druid chants again and new missiles are launched. It looks like we are hurling stones of fine wool, but then I see how on impact they become undone and hundreds of small snakes are released and wriggle through the gaps in the shields so that in no time at all the shield roof is abandoned and the soldiers are fighting to remove the snakes from their helmets, their hair, their clothes. For a moment there is chaos and our spears and shot turn the air black. Once they are no longer in formation, they make better progress up the slope that is treacherous as ice. Nonetheless I am impressed. The roof of shields is a clever trick that we could learn from. Further volleys of slingshot follow and men go down. There is now less than an arm span between the front ranks of the enemy and our own warriors. When they make contact, the clash of weapons makes the hillside tremble.

'Ready, girl?' I nod and Ger and I let fly our spears. My eye follows the powerful arc of mine and I am gratified that it hits home. I am a warrior still.

Somehow we have caused a breach in the Roman wall of shields and now the battle truly begins. Men still sound their battle cries but I can also hear the grunts of effort, the thwack of sword against wood and the other sounds that haunt my dreams – the anguished cries of the dying. I do not listen to them. Instead, I think of what I must do when the enemy breaks through. It does not take long. As I feared, too many of our men are packed together too closely and make easy targets for the disciplined advance of soldiers used to working as a unit. It is as well that Caratacus chose the ground so carefully for with the hill fighting on our side we are not slaughtered in our droves. Even so too many of our men are falling and the silver tide, acting against nature, flows uphill.

I am ready. Those in front of me are not doing well and the wall of enemy shields is building again as I watch. That is a mistake. We have to disrupt them, isolate them. Man for man we are a match for them. When we give them the chance to unite, each man is more than a man and we cannot win. I risk everything by abandoning my secure battle station and launch myself into the madness. They must not prevail.

The ground is treacherous, slick with mud and blood and other things I prefer not to consider. I almost slip and am steadied by a comrade. There is no time to thank him in words, instead I skewer a foe before his gladius sheathes itself in my comrade's guts. We'll call that quits. I hack blindly at whatever comes towards me, kick at shields, and scream till I have no voice left. It is hard labour. I could not have coped if the goddess had not gifted me with my old strength. In spite of it, my arm is tiring quickly. Suddenly I hear a howling of wolves. Hope flares only to die again. I can't see Morcant. I don't have time to look for him either. I scrabble out of the reach of a spear, slide a little and find myself under a Roman shield. I stab my way out, hamstringing an enemy, then crawl away before his comrades can reach me. The man beside me cheers, until a blade slices through his throat.

There is no end in sight. The silver river flows on and I dare not look up to see how Ger fares, for any loss in concentration will see me dead. Another hail of stones gives me a moment's respite as the Romans lift their shields and my blade finds the small weaknesses in their armour at thigh and armpit, at throat and at knee. I thank the gods that I am quick and light enough to leap backwards out of the way of reprisals. I cannot go on much longer; my luck is stretched thin and will surely snap like an over-used belt strap. I am dripping with sweat and breathing hard; my right arm is made of lead. If I am hit, I've not yet felt it. Sometimes warriors die of a wound they have not noticed in the thick of battle. I thrust and hack again, find soft flesh with my blade, stop my ears to the screams of agony, withdraw my sword only to swing and slash with it anew. I don't look at the men I fight. I don't think. I keep breathing, keep looking for an opportunity. I don't worry too much about my defence. I cannot survive this, but the more I kill, the fewer there are left to kill my comrades. The Gwyn of memory no longer chides me but encourages me on. It is tempting to breathe out my fire, but too many of my own side would burn. Fire does not discriminate between friend and foe. I fight on the only way I can: the hard way with sword and shield and will-power. I won't give up. The men struggling to engage me are stumbling over the bodies of their fellows. I won't give ground. I'll stand firm until the horns sound to withdraw. The horns do not sound.

Suddenly I am aware of a new presence, a new force beside me. I look up as best I can while ducking a spear and thrusting with my shield arm to deflect a sword blow. The men before me take a step backwards. I press the advantage. I have no strength left for my war cry and this fight goes on to the rhythm of blows and small, breathless gasps of effort, the music of death. The snarl from my companion sounds loud in this near silence. A man screams and I am splattered by blood. I wipe it from my eyes with the back of my hand. Morcant has arrived.

I can't spare any time to greet him. We are in the middle of the fighting now and in danger of being surrounded. To right and left our line has broken and the Romans are surging forward and upward. We need to withdraw. Someone cries the order.

'Back!'

Our enemies are retreating only to regroup out of the reach of Morcant's jaws and my sword. We have done better than most, but we have moments to avoid being engulfed. Morcant, my ghost of a companion, sees the danger and the wolf pushes me with his great head to drive me up the slime-slick slope. Without his solid four-legged sturdiness I would fall. My leather boots lack the hobnails of the Roman enemy and I keep slithering backwards. I put my arms around the wolf and together we run for the higher ground. Morcant urges me on. His arm is on mine. I almost give up. The Romans are pouring up the hill, more than I can count, more than I can ever kill. Then the horn blows to retreat and I let the wolf guide me away from the battle scene. I think I see Ger limping but still alive, heading for the fortress and his Bethan. I hope it is Ger that I see. He is almost there, at the highest point, and men are leaning down to haul him and the others with him up into the steepest part of the hill, behind the stone wall of the fortress. I'm glad for him but I won't be following him. Caratacus urged us to save ourselves, to run back to our homes. I have no home but I run anyway, keeping pace with the wolf, putting miles between us and the stink of the battlefield. I've done my duty. Now I am free.

CHAPTER THIRTY-TWO

Trista's Story

The wolf could run for ever but even fear of being caught by the Romans can't keep me going for long. I'm alive but that is about all that can be said of me. I'm beyond exhausted.

We stop by a tributary of the great Sabrina. I wash away the grime of battle from myself and from my sword. I inspect for wounds and drink deeply of the clear water, blessed by the goddess. I am uninjured. It hardly seems possible. I check Morcant too. His coat is matted with gore, which he permits me to wash off, but he himself is fine. I thank the gods we have both survived. I sing one of my tuneless little hymns of thanks and cut my palm as I've done before so that my blood can feed the earth. When I wash my hand, the cut heals at once. The goddess of the river is still my ally. That is the good news. The bad is that I have no idea what to do now. No idea where to go.

Morcant is still the wolf.

'I don't know what to do to make you change, Morcant,' I say when I've caught my breath again. He lies down beside me as I squat by the river in the last of the day's sun. I feel the warmth of his flanks against me. He licks my bare arm. His yellow eyes are bright with all the intelligence of the man and I have to fight back tears. There is nothing I can do. Morcant the man looks disconsolate, desperate even, and I know without being told that he fears he will be trapped in wolf form for ever. I can't reassure him. I know that he will transform again, because he has to: in my vision I see him die as a man. I keep that to myself.

We rest for a while near the river in a protected spot. The wolf falls asleep quickly and I doze for a time. I ache in every limb. I don't have any visions, which is a blessing. Maybe my eyes have seen all the horror they can comprehend for one day. My head is clear and I see only what everyone else sees, or so I believe. I like that.

In the late afternoon we walk on through the marshes and cross the rugged hillside of these wilder parts of Alba. There are other tribesmen retreating too, a steady flow of moving men. The enemy have not yet given chase. In any case the landscape favours the hunted, not the hunter. Several men raise their shields in acknowledgement of a fellow warrior but everyone keeps their distance from the wolf.

I think back over the battle scene. There were a lot of dead but many of them were Roman and, of the tribesmen, most of us got away. It was not a noble victory but nor was it an ignominious defeat. Caratacus chose his battleground well and the Romans are now deep in tribal territory. There will be other Roman losses, I'm sure. Once here, they will be at the mercy of raids and ambushes, night-time attacks and mysterious fires. Fewer will leave the territory of the Ordovices than arrived here. This will be a different kind of war.

Just before dusk we meet the other Brigante. They have carts and livestock as well as their women and children with them. Bethan recognises me and runs to greet me, ignoring the wolf as if he were not there.

'We are going to join Idris and his family and settle out west with the Deceangli tribes. There is some land there we can farm and we can keep up the fight. Come with us.' She sounds excited, almost hysterical with relief that Ger survived. And Ger did survive. He is limping and leaning on a staff but hurrying towards me as fast as he can.

'Trista, cariad. I told Bethan you were safe, but she didn't trust me. You fought well. You deserve a feast. Join us. We are going to camp here for the night. You'll be safe with us.'

I hesitate but when I look at the wolf I can see that Morcant the man is beginning to sleep and it is the time of the wolf. He doesn't have to tell me that he has to return to the she-wolf. I see it in his stance, the angle of his tail, the tilt of his head, the look in his eye. Perhaps I'm beginning to speak wolf or perhaps I just have an understanding of Morcant. I pat his back as if he were one of my father's dogs.

'Go,' I say. 'I'll be all right.'

I watch him leave. When will someone run to me with such eagerness, such joy? The she-wolf is the lucky one. I try not to mind. It is Bethan who puts her hand on my shoulder. I am ashamed that I have to blink back tears.

'He has to be with his own kind, cariad, and you must be with yours.' I know she is being wise in her way, but the she-wolf is not Morcant's own kind and Bethan and Ger, for all their loving kindness, are not mine. They are not touched by the gods, blighted by gifts they would be happier without. I have more in common with a wolfman than with them. They are good people and do not deserve the abrupt reply that is forming on my lips so I bite it back.

'You do me honour,' I say, though my voice sounds thick as if choked by the things I can't say. 'Thank you.'

I am greeted as an old friend by Ger's people. I keep forgetting that they watched over me all the days of my sickness after I nearly consumed myself with fire. I struggle to remember that they know me perhaps too well when I don't know them at all. They make space for me by their fire, comment on the length of my hair, my prowess in battle, the beauty of the scabbard that Caratacus gave me. They note every difference in me as if I were one of their children and could not be prouder of me if I were. I am warmed as much by their affection as by the fire and I lend the fire a little more heat of my own in gratitude.

It is both a celebration and a wake, for they lost men in the fray and were not able to collect their bodies. They drink to the dead and then to the living. They cry and laugh and sing and then drink again. I cry too, silent, salty tears, but I don't drink much. I am afraid of what I'll see if I close my eyes.

After a time I sidle away from the fire to a quiet spot on my own. I take a small bone beaker of wine with me. No one comments as I slink away, though I'm sure my retreat doesn't go unnoticed. They are not my family. They treat me like a daughter but my family are all dead. If I half closed my eyes around Ger's fire, I could almost believe I was at home, but I'm not. It is almost harder to sit round his fire than it was to lie in the cold of the Chief's hall. I miss my own people more than ever before. I thought that wound had healed, but it hasn't and my tears are for them and for Cerys rather than for the recent dead. I take a sip from my beaker and then pour the rest of the wine on the ground, a libation in their memory and in memory of the enemies whose lives I took today. I can still see their faces. I shut my eyes and try to banish their images to the storehouse of horrors in my head. The hairs rise on the back of my neck and on my forearm and I shiver. The gods are watching; I can feel it. I sense the intense gaze of a thousand unseen eyes.

Knowing that I'm watched without being able to see the watchers is making me jumpy. I take out Ger's arm ring and immediately the untamed starlit land is alive with the Wild Weird. I have rarely seen so many. They float and flap through the air, crawl and slither at my feet. If they were observing me before, they look away now and go about their own incomprehensible business.

I watch them idly for a while. I know that something is going on, that someone is coming, by the scuttling of the many-legged Weird and the sudden excitement of the flying variety. I unsheathe my sword. I see a small party of cloaked figures a few moments later. One takes the lead and approaches me. There is little light so far from the fire but I can see that he wears a blood-stained cloak of Keltic make. I presume it is another survivor from the battle on the hill. Still I don't sheathe my sword.

'It's a fine blade you have there, and a finer scabbard.' I recognise the voice at once.

Caratacus.

'Sir?'

He lets his cloak fall back and I see that it is indeed the King. His face is as pale as the moon and he is bleeding from a head wound. I leap to my feet to help him to the fire, and call out to Ger and Bethan, but he shrugs me away.

'I'm glad you survived. I heard you acquitted yourself admirably and the earth ran red where you fought. The shapeshifter joined us too, I understand, and added more carcasses to your butcher's tally.' I'm amazed that the King should know so much about so small a part of the battle and wonder how he came by such information, but there are much bigger questions to answer.

'Sir, why are you here?'

'When the line broke – as I suspected it might – it broke so quickly that the high citadel was overrun and my wife and older children taken in an instant. My men urged me to escape and I have left most of them to free my family.' He runs his hands through his hair, leaving a trail of blood. He looks defeated. 'The Romans were looking for me so I swapped cloaks with a tribesman and made my escape. I don't know if I did right.'

Kings of Caratacus' status never let their doubt show; whatever they do is right, for who is to gainsay them? I can't answer him. Perhaps all we can ever do is the least wrong at the time.

I'm about to say something of that sort when I hear the unmistakable cry of a baby.

'What?'

'My son's wet nurse took him and ran when the Romans broke through our defences. She found me and I've been looking for someone I could entrust with his care until such a time as I've rescued his mother and . . .'

He may be a King but he is also a man and I reach out to touch his shoulder. I hear the rasp of metal as a sword is lifted from its scabbard. I do not shift my hand. Even a King deserves some human comfort.

'I didn't know what happened to the child, not till now, but I have seen him in the arms of a loving foster mother. I foresaw it months ago. I didn't know the child was yours!'

'He has to be brought up in the ways of our people, kept safe from the canker of Rome.' Caratacus is babbling, exhausted, overwrought. He puts his hand over mine and I squeeze his shoulder reassuringly. I withdraw my hand and the guard who stands behind the King lets his sword slide back into its sheath.

'That will be so,' I say, 'but now you must come to the fire and eat.'

It is not my place to offer hospitality, but Ger would be horrified if the King was left unwelcomed. He and Bethan are hurrying over to me now. The King looks at me with a kind of wild-eyed hope. 'You know who will care for my son?'

It is only when Bethan takes the child from his nurse that I am certain. Then there can be no doubt. She holds the baby tenderly in her arms and it is just as I saw her in my vision. She and Ger will raise the child to manhood, I'm sure of it, and he will wield the sword that was briefly mine.

CHAPTER THIRTY-THREE

Trista's Story

After the King's mounts and men are fed and watered and the King has held court at the fireside for a time, he brings a jug of wine and joins me in my quiet spot away from the others.

I think he is a little drunk, or perhaps he is merely exhausted. 'I would ask something of you, Trista,' he begins and my heart sinks.

'Of course, sir . . .' I cannot argue with a King.

'I am going to Cartimandua to ask her in person to send your compatriots. Without her forces I cannot trap the legions west of the Sabrina where the land favours us and where the gods are on our side . . .' His words make my stomach churn with apprehension. I don't think he should go anywhere near the Brigante Queen. Every instinct cautions against it. I am about to interrupt, but he stops me with a raised hand.

'Hear me out. I know there are risks and for that reason I

charge you with the safekeeping of my son, and of my story. Watch over him for me and make sure that whatever else happens, when the time comes, he knows his heritage.'

Of all the things I thought he would ask me, I didn't expect this, and of all the responsibilities I was prepared to accept, this is the one that suits me the least. I am a warrior and a seeress, not a nursemaid.

'Sir, if that is what you command me, then that is what I'll do, but please do not go to Cartimandua. In all my dreams I have seen you bound, in chains, and handed over to our enemies. Why would I have such dreams if not to warn you, to save you from such a fate?' My mouth is dry. If he and the Queen are kin, which they may be for all I know, he might cut my tongue out for disloyalty: royalty sticks together when they are not at one another's throat. I take a deep breath. 'Sir, I believe the Queen will choose Rome over you. She will betray you.'

I see anger in his eyes and note that his hand strays to his sword. The Wild Weird are suddenly still and watching.

'You cannot know this for sure? Without Cartimandua's forces we cannot win. If the soldiers of Rome are allowed to advance further west to take Mona, the Sacred Isle, then we'll be broken.' He sounds furious, desperate. 'We have to trap them here while they are still among the Ordovices. The freedom of our people depends on it!' His hand stays on his

248

sword, but he does not draw it and I do not reach for mine; he is a King after all. 'You are telling me I must fail. You are not a druid – why should I trust your words?'

I am a little angry myself. I do not endure what I endure to be called a fraud or a liar. 'My father was chosen for a druid's path and rejected it. He would not have me follow a way he rejected. But trained or not, I am a seeress. I've often wished that I'm not!'

He runs his hands through his hair and rubs his face as if he were a weary, frustrated farmer facing a field of spoiled crops. 'Trista, it's not that I don't believe you are speaking the truth as you've seen it, but I have to go to the Queen. She is our only chance of success. I have to hope that you are a worse seeress than you are a warrior.' My eyes stray towards Bethan and his child. I foresaw that. Caratacus follows my gaze and sighs. 'If you are right, I have not much time. Listen and remember what I tell you so that you can tell my son.'

He wraps himself in his cloak and settles down to tell me his story. He has a druid's skill and I can see his life unfold in vivid pictures in my mind's eye: the wealthy heir, the brilliant war leader and the inspirational fighter for freedom. It is good to have other images in my mind besides the one that has haunted me all my life: Caratacus the prisoner. Why have I been so haunted by his image? Was there something else I was supposed to do to save him?

CHAPTER THIRTY-FOUR

Trista's Story

We talk until dawn and then I persuade him to let me ride as escort with him for a time. Caratacus has more to tell me I think, and is easily persuaded that his child is safe with Bethan, Ger and the slave who saved him in the first place. We ride a little ahead of his other men. We ride cross-country, through rough land, over bare hillsides by ancient forest. The place is thick with the Wild Weird and with the old gods too. Have they retreated here as we have done?

'Don't ask me to settle with Ger's men,' I beg him, for our relationship has changed in our long night of talking. 'I will visit your son and make sure he's safe but I don't think I can live that clan life again. I would be more use fighting with the Ordovices.'

'I charge you with his care. Fulfil that charge as you see fit. I trust to your honour, Trista. Whatever happens, do not let the tribes forget that we fought the invaders, that we have it in us to be free.'

At noon we find a place to camp. We share a meal and then he gets to his feet and embraces me as a father might a daughter. He hands me his seal ring – a ruby, large as a quail's egg. 'Keep this for my son. May the gods bless you, Trista, and remember me.'

My eyes fill with tears at his farewell and to my surprise the Wild Weird who have followed us as if by accident turn as one and bow to him. I know he is riding into my nightmares, into betrayal and humiliation, but I have done all I can to warn him. I cannot do more.

I ride back towards Ger and Bethan and my new responsibility with a heavy heart. I'd hoped to be free.

I don't have Morcant's extraordinary senses, but I have good instincts and I have not been riding for long when I grow certain that I am being followed. I rearrange my cloak so that I can reach my sword more easily. There is nothing more that I can do to protect myself against attack, but slip my armband off my arm and offer my earnest prayers to the gods. I am suddenly on battle alert, riding more cautiously, getting ready to defend myself. The Romans will be looking for survivors of the battle.

It grows darker. Clouds the colour of sable cover the sun and the chill seeps through my thick cloak and into my bones. There is no doubt now that in the silence that precedes the storm I can hear the thundering of other hoofs. This borrowed mare is a fine, hardy little beast but not built for speed; if I am chased I am likely to be caught. My best hope seems to lie within the looming forest. I slip from my mount, soothing her with soft words, and lead her into the trees.

It is so eerily still that I am afraid. The darkness threatens to swallow us up, but my mare is placid as well as hardy and keeps moving where I would hesitate. We are entering another realm; my skin prickles and I shiver. I rest my hand on the pommel of my sword for my defence. There is no wind and even the birds are silent. I bring the mare to a halt and she bends her neck to crop the sparse grass. She seems unworried by the odd atmosphere, but I cannot bring myself to step further into the hidden depths of this forest. I am not yet brave enough to see what lies there so I keep the arm ring in my belt pouch. I want the birds to sing. It is as if everything, even the gods themselves, are waiting.

I listen, straining. Sounds carries well in this uncanny, grey world. Even my feeble senses can detect the thunder of several ponies, ridden hard; the sound of their hoofs is crisp and sharp as a drumbeat. I take out my sword. It feels leaden in my hand. Distantly I hear the first rumbling of real thunder, like the deep throaty growling of a wolf. I am cold but my palms are sweaty and I have to wipe them on my cloak. I can hear voices now, speaking my own language, urgent and ill-tempered.

'Are you sure it is her? I am not riding all this way on a whim.'

'Lord. Hers is a face I will never forget and both my eyes are sharp.'

The chill in my bones threatens to freeze my blood. I know who pursues me: the pedlar I tried to kill and the Chief I partially blinded. So I *did* see the pedlar in the throng before the battle. I ought to have guessed that neither of them would let me go. We are bound together. My heart starts to pound faster than the horses' hoofs, losing all rhythm as if it is about to fail.

I fear that the Chief has brought an entourage, his surviving war band, as well as the pedlar. None of them has any motive for killing me swiftly or cleanly. I did not make things easy for them when last we met. I know the Chief's nature and he will enjoy making me suffer. Should I run or should I stand? That old, familiar quandary. The decision is taken from me when Lugh himself decides. The thunder booms like the god's own voice and a moment later forked lightning cracks open a fissure in the cloud. Such a quantity of rain falls from its broken body that I could believe the grey cloud a dam for some heavenly lake. Heavy raindrops patter then pelt the ground. My pursuers bring their mounts to a halt. It is hard to see an arm's length in front of me in the downpour. I hear them follow me into the wood for shelter.

Icy rain soaks my shawl and so I remove it. It will get in my way and it restricts my vision. I take off my cloak too – it is better for riding than for fighting and I need my hands to be free. My hair is plastered to my head and when I shake it out of my eyes raindrops fly in all directions. I would not be any wetter if I had swum my way to this forest.

The earth of the forest floor is softening to mud and, in hollows, puddles form. This is not good for me. I rely on nimbleness and speed in battle. The clay mud weights my feet as if the earth wants me buried here, and when I finally manage to move the ground is as slippery and unreliable as ice. Perhaps it is the will of the gods that I should die here at the hands of my old enemy? That Caratacus' tale shall never be told and his son live his life without the protection of my sword.

A wild wind whips up from nowhere, bending the trees like bows and setting their branches thrashing. The whole forest is alive with movement and for a moment I fear that the spirits of the wood will turn on me for trespassing on their holy ground. I feel that I am not alone and when I turn to see what horror I must face, I see the bright yellow eyes of the wolf watching me steadily through the driving rain and storm-grey gloom. It is Morcant. Behind him, cowering a little from the driving rain, is the she-wolf.

Some strange blockage forms in my throat that feels like it might become the beginnings of a sob, but I don't let it go.

We look at each other without words for a long moment. His yellow eyes are hard to read and then he comes to stand beside me, just as my enemies crash through the wood on a tide of bad-tempered oaths. It takes them a moment to see me lurking in the shadows, shrouded by the sheets of rain. Then Morcant growls and my enemies' eyes are on us. I hesitate. How should I engage them? There are only four warriors plus the pedlar – it had sounded like more. The Chief, his missing eye covered by a leather patch, roars and slides from his mount. He has the weight of numbers on his side and doesn't need to waste time thinking of a strategy. He runs towards us, pulling out his sword, but the ground is treacherous and he falls. I hesitate but Morcant does not. He is there in two sure-footed, four-legged paces and I know that the Chief is finally doomed. His sword has fallen from his hand and lies out of reach, half buried in the soft grey mud. As Morcant's teeth find his flesh, the Chief screams a cry, equal parts anguish and rage, then Morcant has torn out his throat before he has a chance to raise his sword. The Chief's men are seconds behind, but they pause at the sight of the massive wolf feasting on their leader. Morcant's muzzle and fur is bloodstained and when he bares his teeth they too are red. Careful to avoid the Chief's fate, I don't run but stride cautiously to Morcant's side.

'This is not your fight,' I shout against the roar of the rain and the grumble of thunder. 'Can you not see that our gods are against this? What greater sign do you need?' I think that the Chief's two men would withdraw. I recognise them. These are the men that we have fought before. They have not forgotten that exchange. They believe that if they try to fight me they will die: I see it in their eyes. I can see them weighing up this chance to leave with their honour still intact. Their hands hover over their sword belts. They do not relish this fight. This is a place for the gods, not for men, and all sensible tribesmen know it.

I had all but forgotten about the pedlar. He hates me: I see that at once. I injured his pride and that is not something a tribesman ever forgets. He emerges from behind the horses, brandishing his sword; a finely made blade. He too has to yell against the noise. His fair skin looks almost luminous in this eerie light and his clothes cling damply to his lean and wiry form. It is as if he is a spirit of the forest, a lithe wild-man. I have seen him like this before – in my visions. I have seen him just like this, like an avenging demon, his red hair dark with rain streaming on to his shoulders, his furious face. My guts twist. I know what is coming.

'I will not be bested by a girl!' His cry is more of a savage scream. The sky grows darker. I think it is his intention to face me in single combat. I suppose he hopes that the other men will take care of the wolf, though I would not be confident of that were I standing in his shoes. The pedlar takes a bold step forward into the open space between the trees, no more than a couple of paces from the fallen Chief and the bloody wolf. I don't move. I am like a creature made of stone, held captive by a sense of dread. My sword arm is by my side, my hand is nowhere near my sword's hilt. I know that the men are watching me in surprise, expecting me to respond to the pedlar's challenge. I can only stand and watch him.

And then it happens – as I have seen it in my dreams. He raises his sword above his head and through the slate-black sky, Lugh's lightning finger strikes him down. He does not even scream but falls to the ground, his body blackened and smoking, his face frozen by death into an expression of shock. The Chief's guard do not hesitate but scrabble for their mounts and flee. My gift, it seems, has not left me. The pedlar is dead.

CHAPTER THIRTY-FIVE

Morcant's Story

My pack is complete again. I have found the female who smells strangely of man scents. When she sees me, she bares her teeth in the face, not as a threat but as a sign that she is glad that I am here. My mate does not like it. She hangs back and when it comes to the fight, she waits in the shadows. I know she will come to add her sharp teeth to the fray if I have need of her, but she has little love for men and the long, sharpened tooth they carry that slices our flesh. My she-wolf has little love for the female.

The big man with only one eye is clumsy. I have smelled his stink before and when he falls I know that I can finish him without risk. I don't know what happens after. I don't know why the air smells of burning flesh even when there is no fire, but I know the scent of fear when I smell it and the rain itself is flavoured with it when the men take their horses and run.

We leave too, my pack and I. My two-legged female walks in front with the horses, who might be our prey in other times. We hang back and find shelter from the rain. The two-legged one rides on ahead but her scent is so powerful we know that we can find her again whenever we have need. I do not like the stink of men, but the scent of the two-legged female is good for my nose. She smells of safety and home and these are important things. We will not leave her again.

CHAPTER THIRTY-SIX

Trista's Story

Morcant the wolf and his she-wolf keep their distance but I know that they follow me still. Morcant is still the beast and shows no sign of transforming. I cannot see the man in him, however hard I look. He has no spectral shadow and yet even as a wolf he remembers me. Even as a wolf he saved my life.

I'm glad that he remains a wolf only because that means it is not yet his time to die.

Our encounter with the Chief has brought me two spare mounts and I have plenty of food, enough to keep me for several days should I lose my way. I leave the gods one of the Chief's gold torques, the pedlar's many bangles and his sword before I emerge from the forest. Once more the gods have bought me safe passage through that dark place. I still dare not face them. I keep the arm ring in my bag. The visions have begun again. I see death and flames and Morcant the man lying in a pool of blood. I don't need to see the Wild Weird as well.

By late afternoon it is clear that I am right to be worried. I am being pursued by a unit of Romans. I have been careless of my tracks – thinking the wild landscape protection enough: my ponies churned up the mud enough to be obvious to the least gifted of trackers. I swear volubly. Are the gods only playing with me, using me for some sport of their own? The wolves are nowhere to be seen, which is as well. I don't want them used as target practice by some over-enthusiastic Roman spearman. I hope they will stay out of the way and raise their litter in peace once I am dead. The she-wolf is pregnant; the signs are unmistakable. My only hope is that she gives birth to true wolves. How must it be for a man to be trapped in animal form? Perhaps it is best for Morcant's sake that the man in him is sleeping.

I make my decision: I do not want to be hunted as a wolf pack might hunt a doe. More than that I don't want to lead them towards Ger and the child, my new charge. I will let them get close and fight when I can.

Today the sun is bright in an ice-blue sky. The day is warm and I can smell the scent of pine needles. The wind catches the red cloaks of the riders so that they blow like blood-soaked pennants in the wind, the horsehair crests on their helmets streaming behind them. The light bounces off their breastplates and mail shirts, dances on the polished bridles of their horses, the bright metal of their scabbards. They look magnificent, inhuman: demons indeed. I am not afraid. I rub Caratacus' ring with my fingers. If I cannot tell his story, I will at least die with something of his bravery – as a tribesman should. I dismount. I feel stronger with my feet planted on the ground. I prepare myself to fight and to die. I cannot take down eight men and I don't know if I even have the courage to try.

They have seen me now and their blonde leader vaults from his pony's chestnut back.

I am, of course, bareheaded and the wind whips my tightly braided cords of hair into my eyes and makes them water. I pray to Taranis and to Lugh that I do not falter, that I do not faint or fail to die as bravely as I should.

The blonde officer shouts at me in that barbarous language of his. Though I have no idea what he means, I respond. 'Stay away from me, you half-human spawn of a malformed demon.' Someone laughs and I get the feeling that at least one of their party understands the civilised tongue of the tribes.

I'm right. One of these vile usurpers speaks my language. 'Hey you, woman, I think you should put that sword away. We wouldn't want you to cut yourself.'

I could wish for three more women warriors and we would show him what tribal women can do, but I am alone and I am uncertain that I can give a good account of myself. They have spears and I only have my sword.

'Come and teach me then, you treacherous son of a dog. Let's see if I can't embroider with your guts and spin you a shroud with your hair.'

He translates and the soldiers snort with derision. I can feel my temper rising, but I know it will do me no good to fight angry. I have to stay calm and in control. The blonde man is almost level with me now. He has removed his helmet and is smiling at me. There is something in that smile that incites my fury and I step forward. Almost before I am aware of what I am doing, my sharp-edged blade is at his throat and I have his sword arm twisted behind his back. I move swiftly, abruptly, as I was taught and of course these Romans are too stupid to believe in women warriors, which gives me the huge advantage of surprise. He is as tall as me this man and strong, but my sword is honed to a fine edge and my hand is steady and, if he does not now know that I am a warrior, he is a fool.

'Tell him I will kill him if any of you raise your hands against me!' I shout at the village idiot of a translator. I don't know what to do next. I cannot stay here all day and with no one to relieve me, eventually I will tire. This was probably not my cleverest stratagem.

I had not counted on Morcant. The grass here is long, the

banks of the river covered in shale, and he is skilled at blending into the landscape. It is as if the gods have sent him for my protection, for once more he appears beside me. His snarl sets the ponies to panicking and all the men must dismount to steady them. This is good because they are now, like me, at ground level. They stay back, but I can see them removing their shields from the ponies, preparing to form an unbreachable wall, getting ready to advance.

'Hey, translator!' I call. 'One step forward and the big man gets it!' My sword arm is getting tired. This is not a natural position for me. They know this and are waiting for the moment when I let my sword fall. Suddenly I hear a rush of air and a meaty thwack as a tribesman's spear catches one of the men solidly in the chest. I turn to see the source of the spear and there up on the ridge I see Ger and a war band of maybe twenty men, his own plus Ordovices and Silurians, Caratacus' men!

In moments a full-blown battle is under way. The Romans arrange themselves in fighting formation as the tribesmen charge down the slope of the hill, joyously whooping their war cries. My heart lifts and I find my own rusty voice to yell my own battle cry. The blonde Roman winces at the sound, which is loud and unmelodious – and directly into his ear. I let my sword arm drop and I release my captive.

'Fight like a man,' I say and though he doesn't understand

the words I know he understands the intent because he draws his gladius and attempts to engage me. There is no real contest as my weapon gives me the greater reach and is good for slashing as well as stabbing. He hesitates briefly and lunges forward. He has no shield and his left side is exposed to my longer blade. I don't kill him, merely disable him, slicing at the point on his thigh which is unprotected by his mail. Blood wells and he cries out, but I have only cut through muscle, not bone nor artery. I want him to learn a lesson and remember it: only a fool underestimates a woman. As the pain distracts him, I have him at my mercy. My sword is at his neck. His helmet has rolled on the ground. I have no words he can understand, but I look into his eyes as I pull my sword away, giving him back his life, then I join Ger and Caratacus' men at a run, with Morcant the wolf loping by my side.

It is then that it all goes wrong. A Roman spearman throws his weapon with well-judged force. It arcs towards Morcant. I can see where it must land and I cry out. I am helpless to stop its falling and Morcant is oblivious to the threat. I don't know what instinct brings the she-wolf out of her hiding place in the long grass just at this moment, but I know with the certainty of prophecy that she senses Morcant's danger. She runs at full speed to her mate. I see her accelerate. Even her pregnant belly does not slow her powerful, ground-eating pace and the spear is still falling. It is a frozen moment. I am screaming. I am running too, but he is too far away and I am no sprinter. My cry is lost in the tumult of battle. I cannot make him change direction. And then she is there. I had not known she was so fast. Before the spear can find Morcant's throat, the she-wolf leaps and the spear pierces her side. As she falls, Morcant howls, a sound to turn marrow to ice. I am almost there, but it takes me an age to run to them. I have to leave the fighting to others now. The she-wolf saved Morcant; I have to save her if I can.

The sounds of battle fade and all there is in the world is this wolf and Morcant's anguish. This is not a safe place. Spears are still flying and we are still within range. The she-wolf tries to get to her feet but collapses. She is already worrying at the spear with her sharp teeth. I could wish for something of her spirit and courage but she will not be able to remove the spear without my help, of that I'm sure.

I move forward to inspect the wound and lie down flat on the ground – to make myself less of a target for the spearmen. A glance their way shows me that they are hard-pressed by the tribesmen. As I come close the she-wolf makes a sound in the back of her throat, a warning reminder that I am not her friend. Morcant growls in return. I cannot blame her for being wary of me. The last time she was hurt by a spear, the spear was thrown by my hand. I am in no doubt that she remembers that. She keeps her eyes fixed on me and I sense her suppressed aggression. I get my sword out and she bares her teeth.

'I am going to cut away some of the spear shaft,' I say softly, as if she can understand. She stays still while I saw at the shaft of the arrow with my sword, hacking it off a little way from the head. I may be able to pull the spear out, but the long shaft is awkward and it will be easier to deal with if it is shorter. The she-wolf keeps her eyes on Morcant throughout, as if she needs to look at him to keep from biting me. She is an unusual she-wolf, this one. I can sense how much she wants to hurt me, how hard it is for her to resist and yet she does. The head of the spear is still deeply embedded in her flesh. Carefully, I flatten the thick fur so I can see the skin around the wound. She flinches and snaps her jaws but she does not attack. I wipe away the blood with my tunic. I keep up the kind of patter my father used with the dogs, telling her all the time what I am doing, keeping my voice calm and soft. Some of the metal of the spearhead still protrudes from the wound; these Romans use spear-heads longer than the span of my large right hand, but it is not a hunting arrow and I do not think it is barbed. The she-wolf looks at me again. She is no longer growling but whining. She has no need of words: I know what she wants me to do and what I must do. I remember what I learned from the healer in our hall. When I have pulled out the spearhead, I will need to clean the wound and pack it with something clean. If I am wrong and the spear is barbed, pulling it free might make things worse. My hands shake at the thought, but the she-wolf's fierce look forces me to be strong. I have to take the risk or she will die. Morcant nudges me with his head as if to tell me to hurry. I start to pull at the steel tentatively and the wolf groans. I think this will hurt more if I do it slowly; any attempt to be gentle will only cause more pain. I grit my teeth and pull with all my strength. I feel it budge. The spearhead is not barbed and comes away cleanly. Blood spurts from the wound. It is everywhere, soaking the ground. I use my sword again to cut some fabric from my tunic to staunch the wound. Morcant licks the wound and the she-wolf's nose. His pelt is stained with her blood. I don't know if her unborn litter will have been harmed, if I should try to save them. I have not the skill or the experience to do anything more. I have done all I can.

I leave the two of them together as I run to join the action. I can't help but feel a small pang of jealousy for the closeness they share and for the fact that it was the she-wolf who saved Morcant and not me. I am a seeress and a warrior and yet this female wolf makes me feel inadequate. There is no point in dwelling on such thoughts. I put my energy into my war cry instead. It is clear that for once the tribesman have the upper hand. They have already smashed through the Roman line and are fighting hand to hand. When the line is broken, the Romans are no harder to beat than ordinary men and indeed their swords, as I well know, are less useful in the kind of fighting at which the tribal warriors excel. It looks to be all but over. The blonde commander I wounded is dead and the tribesmen look as if they have little need of an extra sword. I slow to a trot. My eye is caught by a mounted, white-clad figure of a druid some distance away. Is he calling my name? I squint against the bright sun. Even at this distance I recognise him. By some extraordinary coincidence or some god-given blessing, it is the same druid whose fate I foresaw in Ger's village.

I jog towards him.

'What are you doing here?' I ask. Battlegrounds do not demand the same kind of etiquette as formal meals.

He laughs. 'Would you believe that I am looking for you and your companion?'

I don't believe that, but I don't say so. 'I am glad that the fires of my vision have not yet found you.'

His eyes narrow. 'The gods will move in their own time. It is good to see you again. Our gods have blessed you with survival. Times have been hard?'

I nod. Now is not the time or place for lengthy stories.

'Do you have any gift of healing, sir? There is someone I would have you help.' I do not say it is a wolf because I do not want him to turn me down. I help him dismount. He is all bone and sinew, light as a child. I offer him my arm to steady him as he takes a pack from his pony's back and I lead him to where the wolves lie together in the grass.

I hear his sharp intake of breath and fully expect him to berate me for asking him to save a wolf. His response is not what I expect.

There is more blood than I had anticipated. It has soaked through my rough attempt at a bandage and stains Morcant's grey pelt. Have I failed? Is the she-wolf about to bleed to death? Morcant whines, a sound of such sorrow that it tears at my heart.

'Can you help her?' My voice is shaky. I don't know what would happen to Morcant if she were to die. I know that she has kept him safe, helped him to live as a wolf. What if he cannot survive without her?

'Here, give her a few drops of this,' the druid says. He hands me a small pottery vial. Gently, I open her mouth. She allows me to prise open her jaws and drop the liquid on to her tongue. She lets me close her mouth and hold it tight with my hand, so that she swallows the fluid. I find myself humming the tune my father used to sing when he would dose our dogs sometimes with remedies. She does not growl at me this time and her eyes look bright. I think she will be all right.

'What about her cubs?' The old druid touches her carefully, feeling around her abdomen with competent hands. Not only does she not growl but she licks his hand.

'They will be fine.'

'You have a way with animals,' I say and he laughs so heartily I wonder if he has lost his wits.

'Ah, Trista,' he says, 'you still won't see what you don't expect. We'll have to cure you of that.' I am still puzzling over this when he moves to sit beside Morcant. Morcant is watching him with an intentness I have not seen before. He does not snarl a warning, but lets the old man touch the fur on his head, lets him put his scrawny arm around Morcant's brawny back, lets him whisper in his ear. As I watch, the wolf shudders and between one blink of my eye and the next Morcant the man lies there, his skin blue-white with cold, waxy as one dead. His eyes are closed and his body is covered in blood as I have seen him so many times in my heart-rending visions. This is it: I have come finally to that moment that I have dreaded for so long, that I would rather have died than seen. Everything is as it was in my vision: the young man's straggly beard, his long hair spread all round him and his bluish pallor that surely cannot belong to a living man. But his eyes open. He is not dead and the blood that covers him is not his own.

CHAPTER THIRTY-SEVEN

Morcant's Story

My skin feels cool and I am shrunken and naked lying on the ground. Trista is bending over me. Have I been sleeping? The sky is bright and the air is warm and smells of spring. What has happened? I smell blood and when I look down I am covered in it, but it is not mine; it belongs to the she-wolf. She is watching me with loss in her eyes, the flavour of sadness in her scent, and I understand. I have been the wolf, haven't I? But for how long have I been cursed?

Trista is looking at me. She looks terrified. The wind blows her red-gold hair so that she looks like some wild creature of the woods. Her sea-coloured eyes are opened wide with shock and fear and now widen even further with joy. It takes me an instant to understand. She thought me lost to the wolf.

'Morcant!' Her cry catches in her throat so that it seems more of a sob. I feel the dampness of her tears on my human cheek, smell her own unique and special scent through the woodsmoke, mud and forest smells that cling to her. My human arms feel stiff and unresponsive but I find the means to embrace her. I work at my unused human voice and call her name; I spit it out like something that was stuck there, the sound is ugly but she cries the more when I manage to get the word out: 'Trista!'

Her scent floods me with happiness. She hugs me hard and then there are people around her, warriors, and she is taken away from me. I want her to stay.

The old man beside me has his own peculiar smell: not quite man, not quite beast – the strangest stink I have known. I find myself growing wary. Who is he?

'You've been lost, lad.' Something in his voice is disapproving. I've seen him before, haven't I? And then I recognise him. He's the old druid we met in Ger's hall.

'Have you cured me?' My body feels odd and I feel . . . strange. As if I've left a piece of myself behind. I clasp and unclasp my hand in a kind of wonder.

'There is no need to cure a blessing.'

I shiver and he hands me a cloak. Something in his eyes compels me.

'It is a curse. I've been lost, stuck – all this time . . .' I say. How can he know what it feels to wake up in a strange place without clothes, memory, dignity? I last remember the snows of winter and I can see that months have passed and I don't know where I've been or what I've been doing. The she-wolf is hurt and I don't know how.

'It is a blessing. You could have freed yourself any time.'

That makes me angry. 'You don't know anything.' I growl and the wolf is with me suddenly. I am almost overwhelmed by a flood of wolfish thoughts, of sensory impressions. 'If I could have freed myself, I would have done!'

'You are not two but one,' the druid says mildly. 'It is easier to live as a beast than a man. You took the easy way.'

'I am not a wolf!'

'No.' The old man's hand on my arm is as strong as good steel and I am shocked to see the claws beneath his skin. Is he what I am? He holds my arm in a grip so tight it is almost painful. 'You are a man and a wolf together – the best of both.' He snarls and I see the golden shadow of a wolf in his face. He commands me: 'You are the wolf. Remember!'

I do remember then. All of it. All the days when the man in me slept. I remember the night Trista failed in her watch because she was overcome with visions, the days of hunting and the joy of being a creature of instincts and appetites.

'This must never happen again.' The druid's human voice is frail, but the wolf in him is powerful and the wolf in me submits to him.

'Repeat after me: "I am the wolf."'

'I am the wolf.' As I say it, I know that it is true, know it deep within me. Something strange happens then. Something shifts and I feel different, as if I've been a spear warped out of kilter suddenly straightened, a broken sword made whole.

I look down at my own human hand and there beneath my own skin I see the shadow of a silver paw contained within me.

'This is the first lesson. You are one being. One. There are more lessons, Morcant. Will you submit to learn them?' His golden eyes bore into me.

'I will submit,' I say. It is the first time that I've felt at peace since I can remember. I am a wolf and a man in one flesh.

I turn to the she-wolf. She is suffering silently. I reach out to pat her fur, to remind her that the wolf in me is not dead but always here. She is wiser than I am, perhaps even wiser than Trista: she has always known that. She licks my hand. She makes that sound in her throat I know so well. I make a small human attempt at a response. She has lost a lot of blood, but I am not afraid for her. She is so strong.

CHAPTER THIRTY-EIGHT

Trista's Story

Morcant is not dead, nor trapped in the wolf's body for ever! I fall on him like a foolish girl and my tears mingle with the she-wolf's blood and thus anointed he wakes again as a man.

There is not time for a reunion.

I can hear men cheering and shouting and see that the battle is over. Victory belongs to the celebrating tribesmen. The druid calls to Caratacus' men to help us.

The leader is a young man no older than Morcant, with the dark hair and blue eyes of a westerner. I show him my garnet ring. I hear his swift intake of breath and see the pain in his eyes.

'Caratacus has gone to speak to Cartimandua to ask for her help in the fight against Rome.' I pause and see him fight for self-possession.

He speaks quietly, his voice hard to hear. 'It is not over then? She will come?'

The druid looks at me. Should I say more? 'Tell them, Trista. It is as well that they know.'

I hesitate. I can see the hope in their eyes; it pains me to destroy it. 'I have seen that she will betray him. She will hand him over to Rome. The Brigantes will not come.' The men grow silent.

'What else did he tell you, Trista? He gave you something important?' The druid's voice is urgent. I don't think he gave me anything to give these people hope. Without the Brigante, we cannot defeat the army.

'He gave me this ring, and charged me to watch over his son.'

'And?'

'And he told me his story.'

The druid sighs. 'Good. All is as it should be. Did you promise to tell his story, to keep it alive?' I nod. It did not seem like a great burden, not compared to the responsibility for his son. 'Then it is decided. You and Morcant must both come to Mona.'

No! I open my mouth to argue, but he commands here. Three men lift and lay the she-wolf on the shield of a fallen Roman and tie it to the harness of one of the ponies so that she may be dragged along the ground and has no need to walk. Morcant wants to carry her himself, but the druid insists that he does not. I hear the druid promise by the mother, by Lugh and by Taranis that the she-wolf and Morcant will not be separated. He makes Morcant dress in the druid's own spare robe. Morcant's natural colour is returning, and his flesh now looks less corpse-like. I can no longer see the faint silver shadow of the wolf around him, yet the wolf is awake. He has to be. I see it in the confidence of his walk, the assurance of his stance. He lopes towards me, smiling.

'She will be well.'

I love the way his face looks in the druid's white cowl. He takes my hand. It is warm and strong and human and I am struggling for control. I bend his stiffened fingers into a more human shape and clasp his hand as I did before when we travelled together. It seems a long time ago. When I look down, I see the silver paw under his pale human skin and his grey eyes are yellow with the power of the wolf.

This is not how it was. It is as if the wolf is inside him now, no longer a shadow but part of him. 'How? What?' I begin.

The druid is watching us both.

'He has learned his first lesson,' he says and his old eyes are sharp and golden. 'He has embraced his double nature.'

I think I know what he means, but I am still confused. Something is going on that I haven't yet understood.

'I owe you an explanation,' the druid says, and takes my arm as we walk, as if he were my elderly grandfather. It is an honour I could do without. I am wary of druids. Morcant still grips my other hand. The druid continues, 'I knew that you had a rare gift when you came to us that night in the village. Even among druids the gift of true prophecy is rare. You can imagine my surprise when I sensed another presence, another rarer talent with you, his fate entangled with yours.' He pauses for effect as druids do. Is he talking about Morcant? I thought that he'd suspected something. 'I sent Ger to help you as soon as I could and made my own way to Mona – and then to Caratacus. I think you know the road, Trista. Have you still got the arm ring?' I nod and taking it from my pouch slide it on to my arm. I can't help but cry out. Somehow I see within him the form of a great golden wolf. He is surrounded by hundreds of the Wild Weird.

'You see?' I see that he is a werewolf, as Morcant is. I should have seen that before.

'Note how the Weird are drawn to us. Those of us whom the gods bless belong in part to their world.'

Morcant surprises me by adding, 'When I was a shadow, I learned some things about the Wild Weird. They are sustained by the old gods and when the worship of them dies, they die too. That's why they can only live now in the most ancient and sacred of places.'

The druid looks at him approvingly. 'The Wild Weird between them are the soul of the land. We are not just fighting for our tribal territories, but for the summer country, the territory of the soul. If the Romans invade the Sacred Isle, they will destroy everything. The sons and daughters of the tribes will live on, their blood will flow in the veins of their descendants whatever tongue they speak, but the beat of the land's heart will be stopped. We have to remember who we are. Caratacus knows that: his story, the hope of freedom, our pride in who we are, will keep the old ways alive. Stories sustain the soul of the land. His story is worth an army in this other battle.'

I don't know what to say. 'We need you, Trista. We need the things that you can do and the stories you now know.'

I am still overwhelmed, confused. I find myself leaning against the solid bulk of Morcant. I don't ask any of the important questions that I need to know. Instead I just mumble: 'How did you get here?'

'I fought with Caratacus but you both slipped away before any of us could get to you.' I am startled by this and then I remember hearing the howling of wolves. 'Morcant's lived wild for too long. Your talent woke his. The wolf is very strong in him, as the fire of prophecy burns too brightly in you.' He grins and I wonder if he knows about my fire-lighting. 'If I'd not found him, he might have been lost for ever. I have been tracking him since the battle. I'm glad I was not too late. But you both need to come with us to Mona.'

Morcant grips my hand more tightly.

'We have to go there, Trista,' he whispers. He speaks quietly but of course the druid has a wolf's keen ears and interrupts. 'You have made mistakes against our rule, both of you. It was your calling as a seeress, Trista, to warn the Parisi chief of the Roman attack on his fort. You failed in your duty then. Morcant, you lost control of the beast in you and that too is a betrayal of gifts bestowed by the gods. You need to learn what we can teach you. Morcant has agreed to submit to the discipline. Trista, will you too come with me to Mona?'

I know what Morcant wants me to say, but even with the arm ring I know I have not seen all that the otherworld holds. There is darkness there and a strangeness that I am afraid to confront. I've had nightmares about Mona since I was a child. My father, my courageous father, would never speak of it without fear. Dare I go there?

'I promised Caratacus I would watch over the baby . . .'

Ger has joined us while the druid has been talking. He is bloody, but unhurt, and he rests a gory hand on my shoulder. 'But, Trista, I told you – we are going to the Deceangli lands. The Sacred Isle is in Deceangli territory. Me and Bethan and the boy will be as close to Mona as it is possible to be.' I know that he is bursting with pride that he will have the care of Caratacus' son and he wants me to be part of his happy ending.

I can sense Morcant holding his breath. I feel all the skeins of my life and of my visions weaving themselves into shape

281

around me. I am like a spider caught in my own web. So many of my dreams have been about Caratacus, the wolf and Mona. I never thought I saw my own future, but it seems that it has been haunting me for my whole life.

There is only one answer I can give. I take a deep breath. I know that I am making a vow. The Wild Weird are watching me as if my answer matters. The assembled men are waiting for my response and Morcant is willing me to answer. It still comes out as little more than a whisper. 'Yes, I will come with you to Mona.'

Ger hugs me as a father and Morcant kisses me as much more than a comrade. I don't ever want him to stop. I thank the gods for their blessings.

I am Trista. I am a seeress and my visions are true.

Don't miss the amazing Warriors trilogy
also by N.M. Browne

'One of the very best magical adventures
in the past 30 years . . .'
The Times

'She blends history, myth, archaeology and psychology
like no writer I've read since Rosemary Sutcliff'
Independent on Sunday

Read on for the first chapter of
Warriors of Alavna . . .

~ Chapter One ~

Dan watched with horror as Ursula was swallowed by the yellow mist. He tried to call her name, but she didn't stop. He had no choice but to follow her.

It was obvious close to that it wasn't a mist at all in the ordinary sense. He could see moving shapes through it, but they were distorted as if through rippled glass or water. He could not see Ursula. He didn't like it. He took a step forward. The mist enveloped him, colder than ice and oily. It had a surprising solidity. He entered it and it surrounded him; a mass of oily droplets that held him like a fly in a web. No ordinary mist. He shut his eyes instinctively to protect them and took another difficult step. The mist clung to him, resisted his movement. He struggled forward and the mist released him with an almost inaudible pop into some other place. There was no sign of Ursula. He was standing in deserted marshland. It was warm and bright sunlight forced him to squint. There was no sound apart from the twittering of birds. No movement except for the ruffling of the tus-socky clumps of wild grass in the breeze. He looked back; the yellow mist impeded his view of the frozen field he'd just left. Where was Ursula? She had left him at an angry run but even so she only left an instant before him. Why couldn't he see her?

He replayed their conversation in his mind. He hadn't meant to upset her. They had been paired up for the history field trip round Hastings. Miss Smith thought girls kept boys out of trouble – she was an older teacher and must have been due for retirement soon. Dan had never had much to do with Ursula; she hung around with the other misfits in the year group. They were all lumped together in his mind, plain girls, fat boys, the non-starters. Ursula was one of those different ones – she was enormous, over six foot tall, fifteen years old and not just tall but heavy with it. She was solidly built, verg-ing on the very fat. Broad shouldered and long limbed, she disguised her bulk in baggy tops and loose trousers. The effect was unflattering. She towered above her class-mates, a massive cylinder of black sweatshirt and pale flesh. She wore her fine blonde hair very short at the sides and back but hid her cool, blue-grey eyes under a long fringe. Her impassive face was almost sullen. She rarely spoke. He'd been telling her about his training regime. She hadn't volunteered anything, and scarcely answered his questions so he'd set up a steady stream of near meaningless chatter to pass the time. He'd got a trial for the local football club and was a county runner. He'd been showing off, in a half-hearted way and suggested that Ursula tried weight training. He hadn't meant anything by it, but she'd run away from him. The mist had come down while he was talking. He was just about to comment on it because it had merely appeared. To the south everything was unchanged; to the north he could see nothing but the odd yellowness. She had run north. And this was what she had run into ... except that it wasn't. She wasn't here. The marshland offered little cover and Ursula had been wearing a bright red anorak.

It never occurred to Dan to go back without her, any more than it had occurred to him not to follow her. There was a small hill, more of a ridge really, to his right. Perhaps if she had really moved fast she could be behind that hill. She would have had to be a surprisingly good runner, though. Dan began to run too, but carefully, because the ground was uneven and soggy – ankle-breaking conditions. It was strange. The sky was blue here and it was warm. He took off his jacket and tied it round his waist. It was suddenly a beautiful day.

It was not a beautiful day for Ursula. She had run from Dan because she was in no mood for any more jokes about her weight and height. She coped well, mostly, but it had been a bad day. There had been a letter from her father that morning telling her that it wouldn't be convenient for her to visit as planned this weekend because his new baby was sick. This had produced the usual hysterical outburst from Ursula's mother and the usual stoic response from Ursula. She sometimes wished he would give up the pretence of loving her altogether. Dan wasn't really the problem, though she had enjoyed listening to him talk and show off a bit like he did for more normal-sized girls. It was everything really. The Richard twins giggling at the bus stop and some stupid stranger asking her what the weather was like up there. Everything. The mist was a surprise. She hadn't been paying much attention to her surroundings but the mist she couldn't ignore. The colour was sickly, like smog, or like smoke from a witch's cauldron. It clung to her like a fine net, like a cold shroud, freezing the marrow in her bones with its oily touch. She shut her eyes as if she was underwater. Determinedly she strode through it. She wanted to wipe it away, her face felt slick with it and sick with the feel of it. It was not natural, not natural at all. She began to panic. As a toddler she had once got stuck in the small gap under her father's shed. She felt the same fear bubbling now. Then, abruptly she was through it and somewhere else. She heard a pop, like the sound you hear in your ear when the altitude changes on a plane. She was trembling all over and dizzy.

Everything felt wrong. She opened her eyes. Everything *was* wrong.

She was in the middle of a stone circle, surrounded by people. There must have been six men, and a woman, dressed in some historical costume: cloaks, breastplates, strange hairstyles. She didn't really take that in. All but the woman were armed with swords. All of the swords were pointing at her. It could not be real. Her mind rebelled at the evidence of her own eyes. She didn't want to be there. This was not what happened when you were on a history field trip! Ursula was not a coward. Her brain didn't really accept what her eyes told her but her heart did. It began to pump adrenalin at a fearsome rate. She stood up a bit straighter and squared her consider-able shoulders. Trying to control her shakiness, she adopted her 'If-you-mess-with-me-you'll-be-sorry' look, perfected at bus stops and in dinner queues over many years. They were all staring at her so she stared back. She looked at them one by one. Boys often backed down when she did that. These men did not. There was not one of them that did not have the cold hard eyes of a psychopath.

'Oh God!' she whispered in her mind and it was a true prayer.

The woman threw back her head and howled. The sound lifted every hair on the back of Ursula's neck and she shuddered. It was not a sound she would have thought a human throat could make. The men looked discomforted and she noticed one or two grasp their swords a little tighter. The woman began to chant. It was like the sound monks made. In contrast to the unearthly howling, her voice was deep and melodious. It reverberated around the standing stones until the air seemed to thrum with it. It was very beautiful but utterly alien. Ursula felt her body tingling and even her heart seemed to slow to beat time to the woman's chant. It was something more than music, the notes had a force to them that did something to the air. It was as still as the moment before a storm breaks but the very atmosphere felt charged with power. The air crackled as the woman raised her arms and Ursula felt a jolt like an electric shock on the skin of her own arms. What was going on? She strained to hear the woman's words. They were in no language that she recognised.

The woman's voice was becoming more insistent, the rhythm faster, the pitch higher. Then the woman looked at Ursula. It was a very direct look. The woman's eyes were an extraordinary emerald green, intense and searching. They were more frightening than the swords in the hands of the men. But Ursula was used to being afraid and of pretending not to be. She would not give this woman power over her by showing her fear. Ursula stared back implacably, her own eyes as hard as she could make them. The woman gave a little cry of surprise and crumpled to the ground in a graceful and dramatic swoon that Ursula would have been proud of.

The rite, if that is what it was, was clearly over. With the woman's fall into unconsciousness the charged quality of the air ceased at once, almost as if someone had thrown a switch and shut off the current. There was a strange noise, a kind of implosion almost out of her hearing range, that Ursula sensed rather than heard. A couple of the men muttered to each other and pointed. Ursula, swinging round to follow their gaze, half expected what she saw. The mist was gone. Not a wisp of it remained. There was nothing unusual in the view. Beyond the stones there was only flat and marshy land stretching as far as the eye could see. There was nothing unusual about it, except that it bore no relationship at all to where Ursula should have been. There was no sign of Dan or any of her classmates. There was no sign of the car park where their coach should have been parked. There was nothing but the marsh and the standing stones and no one but the men with their swords still drawn.